THE ODDEST LITTLE CHRISTMAS SHOP
&
THE ODDEST LITTLE CHRISTMAS CAKE SHOP

Beth Good

Beth Good

This Special Christmas Double Edition

published by

Thimblerig Books 2016, Devon, England

ISBN-10: 1539710815
ISBN-13: 978-1539710813

CHAPTER ONE

In Which Our Intrepid Heroine Is Mistaken For An Octogenarian

A lone snowflake drifted past her cheek, beautiful and ethereal, then landed gently on her booted foot before melting to nothing. Pippa watched it disappear with a less than enthusiastic expression, then returned to clapping her hands and stamping her feet to keep warm.

Good grief, she thought, *Scotland is freezing at Christmas!*

The Scottish Highlands were picturesque, with misty mountains and snow-topped pines. But there really ought to be a health warning as you pass the border.

Peering up and down the platform in search of Great Aunt Evelyn's wild and bushy hair, Pippa began to despair of ever being collected. But just as she was about to give up and dig out her phone, her bleary vision was accosted by a large white cardboard sign being thrust into the air further down the platform, writing scrawled across it in black marker pen.

Normally she would not have looked twice at a man waving a sign on a platform. Such signs were always for someone else, and besides, she was expecting to be met by her wonderfully dotty great aunt.

But what drew her attention to this particular sign was that it bore her full name in capital letters:

PHILLIPA FRANCES JOY.

Pippa read her name twice before quite understanding, then moved her gaze to the man holding it aloft.

She could not see his face, just the top of his head, warmly ensconced in a thick woollen cap. It was the kind of headwear she usually associated with aging, paunchy fishermen on bar stools in obscure country pubs. Yet below the sign was a broad chest in a dark green sweater and shooting jacket, with what appeared to be flat abs below it. Her gaze dropped lower, admiring a pair of unexpectedly muscular thighs in tight-fitting black jeans, and finally to the muddied green wellington boots that completed his ensemble.

Hmm, she thought, studying his physique with approval. Perhaps Christmas in the Highlands was not going to be that cold after all.

The crowd had thinned, and it took only a few seconds to push her way through to her mystery greeter. 'Hello,' she said saucily, addressing the sign and the invisible man behind it. 'Are you for me?'

The sign was abruptly lowered. Pippa took a step back, suddenly dizzy. Wow, she thought, I hope he *is* for me. He would make a rather splendid early Christmas present.

The woolly cap had not given her a clue that the man wearing it would be quite so drop-dead gorgeous. Tall, dark, and if not handsome, then certainly striking. His nose was slightly too long, and his eyelids too heavy, and that dangerous mouth ... Though he did not look very cheerful, she realised, her smile fading as she met a pair of intense dark eyes that scrutinised her in a most uncomfortable fashion.

His eyebrows slanted furiously, as though about to accuse her of something unpleasant. Then he demanded in very Scottish tones of disbelief, 'Phillipa Joy? You're … Mrs Phillipa Frances Joy?'

He was looking astonished and horrified at the same time. It would have been comical if she had not been so taken aback by his attacking manner.

'Miss,' she corrected him, a little offended. 'And I prefer Pippa, actually.'

He seemed stunned, looking her up and down. 'You're Evelyn's *little elf*?'

'Is that what she called me?' She grinned. 'I suppose that makes *her* Mrs Santa. Though Evelyn's a bit slim for that job. I've always imagined Mrs Santa to be over-endowed, that kind of motherly figure. Not that Mrs Santa is known for having dozens of kids, of course, unless you count all the elves. They could be considered a sort of pseudo-family, couldn't they?'

'But who are you?' he asked abruptly, ignoring her Santa nonsense in a way that reminded her of her last boyfriend.

'I'm her great-niece. I often come up from London to help out at Christmas. Because of her shop, you know. It gets so busy at this time of year.'

'I see,' he said drily. 'When she said *Phillipa Frances* was coming to stay over Christmas, I thought she meant you were one of her old friends. I was looking for a woman in her seventies or eighties.'

'Disappointed?' she couldn't help asking.

'Not at all,' he replied, but she did not believe him. 'I'm sure she'll be glad of your help.'

'She always welcomes an extra pair of hands in the shop over the festive season. Evelyn's not exactly a spring chicken, even if she does still insist on riding that ancient motorbike of hers all over the Highlands. But who are you?' She raked him up and down with a glance herself, suddenly wary. 'I thought Aunt Evie was going to pick me up herself.'

'Evelyn's not been very steady on her feet recently, so I offered to come and pick you up instead.' He stuck out a gloved hand, still unsmiling. 'I'm Ben Shakespeare. Your cousin.'

No way, she thought. No way was he her cousin!

She shook his hand in a daze. He had a firm masculine grip. Rather too firm, in fact. Her already cold fingers felt numb when he released them, as though he had cut off her circulation.

'My ... *what?*'

'Cousin Ben,' he repeated. 'I've come for Christmas too. To help out in the shop.'

'Is that so? The more the merrier, I guess.' But she was surprised. Very, very surprised. For a start, there was zero family resemblance. And secondly she had never heard of his existence. 'Are you staying at her house too?'

'Yes.'

'Right through Christmas?'

He met her eyes. 'Yes.'

'Gosh, won't that be ... cosy!' He was sexy to look at, but *Ben Shakespeare?* No, there was something suspicious about all this. 'I'm sorry, this will sound terribly rude. But I don't ever recall a Ben Shakespeare in the family.'

'I'm a distant cousin. Very distant. Several times removed, in fact. The Canadian branch of the family. I'm not sure of the exact, erm ...' He frowned, and she copied him, struggling to follow his explanation. 'Let's see. My maternal grandfather emigrated to Canada years ago. Then the family got separated ...'

'You don't sound very Canadian.'

His brows shot up. 'Don't I?' he demanded, his voice suddenly very Scottish and aloof, and she decided not to press the matter.

'Well, it's good to meet you, Ben.' *Whoever you really*

are, she finished in her head. She hesitated, then tried to sound more cheerful. 'Merry Christmas!'

'Christmas,' he grunted in reply, his eyes narrowing. 'I've never liked Christmas. All that enforced jollity, and Santa with his wee elves. And now I'm surrounded by it, day in, day out.'

She was surprised. 'You don't like Aunty Evie's Christmas Shop? But why offer to help out, then?'

He ignored her question, reaching for her suitcase. It seemed the pleasanteries were at an end. 'May I help you with your case, Phillipa?' he asked brusquely, picking it up anyway as though her permission did not particularly interest him.

'Be my guest. But it's Pippa.'

'We've got to hurry. The car's parked across the road. There's a subway.' He strode away without waiting for her. 'Follow me.'

Cousin Ben moved swiftly through the crowd of Christmas travellers, carrying her heavy case as though it were packed with feathers. He was surprisingly adept at manoeuvring round or over multiple obstacles of cases and trolleys. She followed more slowly, admiring the old Victorian station as always, the high iron rafters of its entrance hall dominated by rows of hanging golden stars and silver snowflakes. Below them stood a vast Christmas tree festooned with flashing lights and baubles, with fake presents in Christmas wrap round the base. It was all rather lovely and festive.

Despite her moaning about the weather, she secretly loved visiting Scotland, it was a real treat. But the wind whistling through the station was still savagely cold after the stuffy warmth of the train.

'Try to keep up, would you?' he threw impatiently over his shoulder.

'In a hurry?'

He shot her an unreadable look. 'I don't like leaving our aunt alone for long. She's been … frail, lately.'

'Oh poor Aunty Evie. I knew she'd hurt her ankle, but I didn't realise it was so serious.'

Guiltily hurrying her steps, Pippa rummaged in her coat pocket for a pair of fur-lined leather gloves and drew them on. It had been cold in London this week, but nothing this bitter. It had been snowing in the Highlands all month, the fields she had seen from the train white with snow, and although it was not snowing at the moment, apart from the odd wayward flake, she guessed the weather was not about to improve. So it would be gloves and snow boots and hot toddies for the next fortnight.

Ben wasn't friendly, but he was definitely in the eye-candy category. Not a bad way to spend Christmas, she thought, risking an assessing glance at the man striding ahead of her. She wondered why he was pretending to be her cousin, and had just begun to spin a naughty little daydream around the two of them relaxing on a fleece before a log fire, hot toddies in hand, when he interrupted her thoughts.

'About the accent thing.' Oh, so he had decided to answer her question, after all. Or had just come up with a likely cover story, she thought suspiciously. 'My mother came back to Britain from Vancouver when I was about ten,' he explained. 'That's how I lost the Canadian accent.'

The snow in the car park had all but turned to slush under the constant traffic of feet and cars. She watched as he lifted her suitcase effortlessly into the back of a muddy old Range Rover which she recognised as belonging to her great aunt. That fact shook her.

He must be telling the truth, she thought, smiling at him mechanically when he threw open the passenger door for her. Aunt Evelyn would never have let a stranger drive her beloved car.

So he *was* her cousin! And Canadian, but with a Scottish accent. What a strange combination.

Either that, she considered, or this man had kidnapped her great aunt, stolen her Range Rover, and was now abducting *her*! Which was highly unlikely, given that Aunt Evelyn was not a wealthy woman. And what kind of thief steals a clapped-out heap like this? None of it made any sense. But she would play along until they reached the shop, at least.

Pippa turned to get into the passenger side and slipped on an icy patch, tried to regain her balance by grabbing at the wing mirror, and merely managed to rip it off, ending up on her bottom in the slush.

'Bloody hell!'

Momentarily she had trouble breathing. Her sudden collision with the ground was not only painful but freezing. Her all-time favourite combination.

Ben came round the car to find her sitting in the slush, clutching a wing mirror. He frowned. 'What on earth are you doing down there?'

'Oh, nothing. I was tired so I thought I'd have a sit down.' She held out the wing mirror to him. 'Here, sorry, take this. Got any super-glue?'

He took the broken wing mirror with a quizzical look, then gave her a hand up. His grip was strong, heaving Pippa to her feet as though she weighed nothing. 'If you've finished vandalising the car,' he said curtly, 'I'd like to get back to the shop.'

'Yes, quite finished.' She shook out her coat, now sodden at the back, and climbed into the ancient Range Rover with as much dignity as she could pretend.

It was colder inside than outside the car, and her bottom felt soggy. She wrinkled her nose. The interior of the car smelled of mushrooms. Fungi was probably growing under the seats. And, despite her first positive impression of his gorgeous physique, her taciturn companion was far from making up for the smell. Oh, this was going to be such fun. Working like a slave all day in the Christmas Shop, then cooped up with this charmer overnight at her great aunt's house. Elves by day, this ogre by night. He would be like the bad fairy at the feast. Only without the sparkly wings.

The bad fairy started the engine and backed out of the parking space, his view no doubt hampered by the liberal amount of mud and snow with which Great Aunt Evelyn liked to decorate her vehicle. Indeed, she had a strong suspicion the Range Rover had never been put through a car wash in its long and undistinguished life. But it was better than walking, she conceded, staring through the grimy windscreen at slushy streets.

'So is your mother living in Scotland too?' she asked, attempting to dig deeper into his mysterious past. Canadian, indeed! He was about as Canadian as she was.

'Who?' Totally blank, Ben glanced at her as though she were mad. Then seemed to click back into their previous conversation, his reply stilted. 'Oh, I see. No, she ... she settled south of the border.'

He answered her questions like someone reading a script, she thought suspiciously. Or maybe a robot. That mental image amused her, and for a moment she entertained herself by imagining he had wires instead of brain cells inside that very handsome head.

Then he ruined her amusement by adding sombrely, 'She's dead now, of course.'

'Oh dear. I am sorry.'

'It was a long time ago. Very sudden though.'

She bit her lip, contrite. 'Heart attack?'

'No, she was hit by a truck.' He paused at a junction and cautiously looked both ways, eyes narrowed as he surveyed the snowy streets. 'A truck full of ... poultry.'

She was stunned, and not quite sure she believed him. 'Poultry?'

'Frozen geese and turkeys, mostly. For Christmas dinners. She was out walking her dog on a country lane. The truck came round the corner too fast. Killed them both instantly.'

'Oh my god. That's awful.'

Cousin Ben nodded, staring grimly ahead. 'Yes, we try

not to talk about it. But Christmas is always a difficult time of year for us.'

'I can imagine.'

Now why would he make up a story like that? She sat in silence for a while after that, having thoroughly stuck her foot in it last time she tried to make conversation. It was a particular talent of hers, she considered. Saying the wrong thing at the wrong time. But it was perhaps better than saying nothing at all, which seemed to be his approach to social intercourse, as her favourite writer Jane Austen might have said.

The snowy countryside flashed by at an alarming rate, considering the icy state of the roads, and more than once she had to clutch at the door handle as he cornered at speed. Good grief, was he trying to kill them? Perhaps he was still thinking of that murderous poultry truck driver.

But at least it was gorgeous scenery. The little Scottish town looked marvellously festive, bedecked with gleaming snow and with Christmas decorations in every window. The town lights had been switched on, with gold and silver stars shining above the shop windows along the old-fashioned High Street as dusk began to fall. Behind the town itself, which lay partly in a valley, rose a forest of snow-crested pines stretching up the steep hillsides to the north. It was really very lovely and Christmassy, and still her favourite place in the British Isles, not least because she had spent so many happy Christmases there since her childhood.

'What kind of dog was it?' she asked at last.

He stared at her blankly again. She tried not to arch her eyebrows. It might not be his fault. Perhaps he had some kind of mental condition which made him zone out in the middle of conversations. Roddy had had an odd habit of doing that too. She struggled not to bare her teeth at the thought of her ex-boyfriend. It had been months since they split up, after all. And he had never been very satisfactory as a boyfriend.

'Jack Russell,' he muttered. 'I think.'

'Poor little thing.'

He grunted something else she didn't catch. Probably something uncomplimentary about Jack Russells.

My cousin Ben is not much of a conversationalist, she thought, glancing at him sideways. But then it must be a very painful subject for him. Both her own parents were still alive, so she had no experience of how it would feel to lose one of them. And in such a brutal manner.

Pippa bit her lip. Had she hurt his feelings by raking over his mother's death? That might explain his cold front.

Her older sister Debbie was always complaining that she never thought about other people's feelings, just opened her mouth and said the first thing that came into her head. Perhaps this would be a good time to experiment with being a more thoughtful person.

Trying to be uncharacteristically sensitive, she pinned a determined smile on her face and directed the conversation elsewhere. 'Shakespeare. That's an unusual surname.'

'No relation,' he said promptly, though she hadn't asked. As though everyone always assumed he must be related to a certain Warwickshire playwright.

'What, of mine?' she teased him, and was rewarded with that fulminating look again, the dark brooding glare from under furious eyebrows. 'Sorry, I was joking. I do remember a Shakespeare in the family,' she lied hurriedly, 'now that I think about it. Definitely, yes.'

He looked back at the road, and she had the distinct impression he was dismissing her from his mind. 'We'll be there soon. It's another few blocks.'

'I remember the way.'

'Of course you do,' he said shortly, making it clear he did not believe her. 'When were you last here? Evelyn said you hadn't visited in some time.'

'Three years,' she admitted coldly, abandoning her attempt to be friendly, and folded her arms across her chest to indicate her disapproval of his attitude. She had been very busy building a career since leaving university, and Scotland was a long way from London. And her sister Debbie *never* came to visit Aunty Evie.

But what with the thick scarf and coat she was wearing, it was actually quite uncomfortable to maintain that disapproving position. It felt like she was cutting off her circulation. She let her hands slip meekly into her lap again, sitting in silence like the mild-mannered pensioner he had presumably thought he was collecting.

He also said nothing more, but his fingers tapped the wheel in an irritated fashion.

Gosh, she thought, watching her cousin, he's a very edgy person. But maybe he just needs some caffeine.

She was often a little irritable until she'd had her first cup of coffee. Though 'irritable' was a bit of an understatement. Some days she bordered on the psychotic. Fresh-ground coffee was her preference, but she could just about stomach a good instant if there was no alternative.

Luckily for everyone in the school staff room, she usually had a few shots of strong expresso early in the morning and trundled off to her classroom with her mental wheels thoroughly oiled. Though with the insane dash to catch her train that morning, she had not managed to ingest any caffeine until well after ten o'clock, by which time she had already snapped at several fellow passengers and a bewildered ticket inspector.

She saw the Christmas Shop looming in the distance, and could not help grinning. There was something about the place that always made her smile. She felt like a big kid when it came to Christmas, and she did not care who knew it. But how gorgeous it looked! Dusk was creeping in, and the flashing reindeer with its glowing red nose and the larger-than-life-size Santa on the roof could probably be seen from the other side of town. Maybe even from the moon. Her great aunt really did know how to put on a show.

'The Christmas Shop!' she exclaimed impulsively, and clapped her hands. 'How I've missed it! It always looks so jolly. And that's a very cheeky smile on Santa's face.'

Ben did not comment. There was always a reserved parking space outside the shop for Aunty Evie's car. He pulled sharply into it without signalling or slowing down first, jolting her forward so violently in her seat that she almost hit her head on the windscreen.

'Sorry,' he said, with an air of total unconcern.

'That's all right. I've always wanted a brain injury,' she muttered, righting herself with difficulty. Her bobble hat had slipped sideways. She pulled it straight, and refrained from snapping at him. Think of the Christmas spirit, she told herself firmly. Merrily, merrily, merrily, merrily …

He turned off the engine and scowled round at her, eyes narrowed on her face. 'Pardon? I didn't catch that.'

'Nothing,' Pippa said brightly, then rummaged down at her feet for her handbag, which seemed to have slid under the seat.

When she straightened up, a little breathless, she found him still staring at her from mere inches away. It was unnerving.

'Here we are then,' she went on, smiling broadly and trying not to make it obvious that she found his behaviour the wrong side of odd. 'Last stop! Everybody off!'

She had handled much more horrible boys at school, after all. Though of course most of them had been under twelve years old, and he looked decidedly older. Though probably only a few years older than her, in fact. Not much beyond twenty-eight, she decided, then dragged her gaze away from his. Gosh, his presence was a little overwhelming at close quarters.

'And the shop does look lovely this year,' she rambled, clutching her handbag to her chest as though she might be called upon at any moment to bash him over the head with it. 'It's wonderfully festive, don't you agree?'

And it was true, she thought suddenly, taking a

minute to admire her great aunt's Christmas Shop. Evelyn had done a fabulous job on the window-dressing this time. The entire shop front was flashing with light, decorated with multi-coloured lights woven around a magical display of candy canes, nodding elves in green and red jackets, a vast treasure chest spilling over with foil-wrapped chocolate coins, and the usual array of beautiful green wreaths, mini-Christmas trees and reindeer costumes in the window.

The door was open and she could hear Christmas music wafting out, a jaunty version of *When Santa Got Stuck In The Chimney* that already had her feet tapping.

Cousin Ben looked past her at the Christmas shop, studying it at length. His face did not change. No doubt unrelenting grimness was his default expression.

'If you like that kind of thing,' he conceded, but did not look impressed. 'Personally, I think it's verging on the garish. All those flashing lights. Not very subtle, is it?'

'Oh cheer up, it's Christmas!'

'Not for another ...' He hesitated, glancing at his watch. 'Eight days.'

'Fine, it's *almost* Christmas.' She tried to sound bracing and authoritative. 'Now come along, let's get inside. It's freezing and I can't wait to see Great Aunt Evelyn again.'

But when Pippa tried to open the car door, she found it was locked.

'Just hang on a second,' Ben said coolly, not looking at her but staring along the shopping street.

She peered down the snowy street too, wondering what he was looking at, but could not see anything out of the ordinary. It was a normal pre-Christmas scene for a quiet Scottish town, in fact. A few hardy shoppers, a man walking a Pekinese, a well-built lady with several bags and parcels in the front basket attempting to get back on her overloaded bicycle ...

'Erm, what are we waiting for?'

Ben did not reply, his eyes still narrowed as he studied the street. He had even placed a hand on her arm, as though to restrain her. She glared down at it. Did he think she was about to break out of the car? Maybe using the crowbar she kept in her handbag for just such situations?

'Ben,' she insisted, using her cross but professional teacher voice, the way that always had such an impact on Year Six. 'Could you unlock my door, please?'

His gaze returned slowly to her face. He did not immediately respond, keeping her waiting while he examined her expression. She had the feeling she was being dissected, like some unfortunate frog in a science lesson, and that soon there would be nothing this man did not know about her.

'You do like to be in charge, don't you?' he murmured, adding in a mocking voice, '*Sergeant Pippa.*'

Her mouth tightened. Bloody cheek! 'In general, yes.'

'Then that's going to be unfortunate for you,' he replied calmly, 'because so do I.'

Panic set in at that. With a tiny touch of fury mixed in. She did not like being bossed about by men. It never ended well, in her experience. It certainly had not ended well with Roddy.

She shook her door handle noisily. 'Let. Me. Out.'

His smile continued to mock her. 'Come on, play the game properly. You want to get out. What's the magic word?'

Her blood pressure rocketed. The infuriating man! It was all she could do not to bash him over the head with her handbag.

'*Now?*'

ODDEST LITTLE CHRISTMAS

CHAPTER TWO

In Which More Than Pippa's Suspicions Are Aroused

Ben Shakespeare looked at her in mock disappointment, shaking his head. '*Please*, Pippa. *Please* is the magic word.'

She took a few pleasurable seconds to imagine this disagreeable man boiling in oil. Then forced herself to mutter, 'Please.'

He smiled, leaned past her and lifted the lock by hand. The car door opened at once and she almost fell out, or would have done if his arm had not been pressed across her chest.

'You must have leaned on the lock,' he said softly.

Her face hot with temper and embarrassment, Pippa pushed him away and climbed out of the Range Rover without another word. What a dreadful man he was! Leaned on the lock, indeed. He had somehow contrived to lock it from his side, then pretended he hadn't.

Striding across to the shop, still glancing back over her shoulder, she collided with the man walking the Pekinese.

The man stumbled backwards, jerking on the poor little creature's lead so hard it must have been half-strangled. The dog yelped, but the man did not even look down at it, glaring at Pippa instead with such hostility that she was almost alarmed.

'Sorry,' she said quickly, and stopped to pat the

Pekinese on the head. It yapped at her and she straightened, more embarrassed than ever. 'Poor doggie. It's my fault, I wasn't looking where I was going.'

'No, you were not,' the man agreed curtly, in a thick Scottish accent. He looked piratical, with a nasty scar across his cheek and a thick gold ring on one of his fingers. 'You should be more careful.'

'Merry Christmas!' she said apologetically as he brushed past her. But the man paid no attention, and he and his dog were soon lost in the swirling snow which had begun to fall.

Pippa felt another snowflake land on her nose, cold and wet, and could have squealed with excitement as though she was still six years old. But of course Mr Miserable was watching, and it was clear he already thought she was an idiot. Instead she allowed herself a happy grin and marched through the open door of the shop with snow on her hat and coat.

Now that she was here in Scotland and snow was falling, it felt like a proper Christmas. She did not even mind the cold so much. Indeed, she was quite prepared to spend the next eight days working furiously hard to sell as many Christmassy things as possible for her great aunt.

There were not many customers in the shop, but there was a wonderfully familiar face behind the till.

'Phillipa!' Great Aunt Evelyn stood up, leaning on the glass-topped counter and gesturing her to come for a hug. 'How marvellous to see you, lass! And covered in snow. You are a good girl, coming all this way just for your old aunty.'

'You know I wouldn't have missed it for the world, Aunt Evie. And do please call me Pippa, I barely recognise my name when you call me Phillipa.' She laughed, hugging her great aunt tight. It had been too long since she had seen her, she decided, cross with herself for neglecting her old Scottish aunty.

Great Aunt Evelyn – or Aunty Evie, as she preferred

to call her – looked trim as ever, even swathed in a knee-length red Santa dress matched with a sturdy cardigan, tissues hanging out of her pockets. Maybe she looked a touch thinner than usual, Pippa thought. And there were dark shadows under her eyes, as though her great aunt had suffered more than a few sleepless nights lately. What could be wrong?

Then she gasped, looking down at her Evelyn's bandaged foot and ankle. 'Oh no, is that your poorly foot? When you said you'd hurt your ankle, I thought it was just a sprain …'

'Aye, and so it is,' her great aunt insisted. 'But Doctor Farley at the clinic is so thorough. He's young and very keen, you know? He insisted I take a few weeks off. But of course how can I?' She sat down again and opened her arms wide, losing a few crumpled-up tissues from her pocket as she did so. 'Look how much stock I still have to sell, and this is my busiest time of year. I run a Christmas shop! It would kill me to close during the festive season.'

'There's absolutely no need to close the shop,' Pippa told her firmly, beginning to unwrap her voluminous multi-coloured scarf. Her mother had knitted it for her last Christmas, and it seemed to go on forever. But it was very warm and cosy. 'Not with me and … ' She glanced round to see her cousin had appeared in the doorway, car key in hand, '*Cousin Ben* to help out in the shop.'

'Cousin Ben?' Great Aunt Evelyn looked flustered, staring past her at her other helper, then nodded jerkily. 'Aye, of course. Such a godsend in my time of need.' She smiled weakly, and Pippa thought she caught a flicker of fear in her eyes. ' B … Ben's introduced himself, then?'

Concerned, Pippa glanced over at Ben. His frown disappeared at once, and he smiled, rather more naturally this time than he had done in the station. 'Yes,' she agreed slowly. 'We had a nice chat in the car on the way over. I had no idea we had family in Canada.'

'Canada? Oh yes, indeed,' Aunty Evie said brightly.

'Lots of them.'

Ben strolled over and laid the car keys on the counter. His smile did not quite reach his eyes, she noticed. 'Everything quiet while I was gone?'

'Oh yes. Perfectly quiet. And you?'

He nodded, watching her, his hand still resting on the car keys. 'The car's running well, Aunt Evie. Apart from a broken wing mirror.' He glanced at Pippa, who flushed with mortification and stammered a quick apology to her great aunt. 'Nothing to worry about. But you'd better let me drive for now. Just in case something were to suddenly go wrong. And no taking out the motorbike instead, not with your bad ankle. Do you understand me?'

Aunt Evie knit her hands together in her lap, gave a quick jerk of her head, then looked up at him mutely. Which was very unlike her great aunt, Pippa thought, watching the two of them exchange a speaking glance. It was almost as though he were controlling her.

'Are you all right, Aunty Evie?' Pippa asked, now very concerned. There was something going on here, she was sure of it. But what?

Ben straightened up, looking round at her sharply. 'What are you talking about?'

'You tell me,' Pippa invited him, feeling ever so slightly aggressive towards this mysterious 'cousin'. Which was also unlike *her*. But there was something not right here and she was determined to get the truth out of one of them. Even if she had to wait to get Aunty Evie alone tonight.

His dangerous gaze narrowed, then slid sideways to Evelyn's nervous face. 'Did I miss something while I was locking the car?'

'No, laddy, I'm fine, honestly,' her great aunt insisted at once, and smiled broadly at them both. 'I'm tired, that's all. Not quite myself. It's been such a very long week. And all because of this stupid ankle. Did Ben tell you … how it happened?'

Ben shook his head silently, still frowning.

'Aye, well, I was on a weekend trip to Glasgow,' Evelyn said, her voice suddenly high and breathless. 'And I fell down some steps coming out of the … erm … one of the museums. So silly of me. But Ben came straight away when I called, took me to hospital, then drove me back here.' She smiled up at Ben in a strained way. 'I don't know how I would have managed without Ben, he's been a perfect poppet.'

A perfect poppet?

'I'm sure,' Pippa said drily.

Ben's mouth twitched.

Aunty Evie hobbled away to serve a middle-aged lady who had come to the till with a gorgeous winter scene snow globe for her grandson, quickly telling Ben where to find the presentation box for it. After she had gift-wrapped the box and thanked the customer, she turned her attention back to Pippa.

'Now, dear, would you like to go straight up to the house and get settled in? I've given you the big back bedroom on the second floor. I hope you won't mind being at the top of the house and not in your usual room, opposite mine, but … ' Evelyn hesitated, glancing at Ben. 'I gave that room to Ben, I'm afraid.'

Pippa was slightly surprised at this, and even a little hurt, but she struggled not to show it. She had not confirmed with her great aunt that she would be coming up until late last week, after all. Maybe Evelyn had assumed she would not be making it this year, and so had given the best guest bedroom to her cousin instead.

Assuming he *was* her cousin, which she was seriously beginning to doubt.

'I don't mind where I sleep, Aunty Evie, honestly. And I'm sure being up a flight will do wonders for my legs. Save me a fortune in gym fees.'

Aunty Evie laughed, looking relieved. 'You don't need to go to the gym, surely? With a lovely figure like yours!'

Pippa stuck her hands on rather less than slim hips. 'Um, sadly, I do need the gym. Not that I make the effort very often. That's what comes of being a school teacher, I suppose. I'm always so exhausted after work, I just flop on the sofa and eat fattening things.'

Ben turned his head, his dark brows jerking together in surprise. 'You're a teacher?'

She nodded. 'Primary.'

Aunty Evie had started folding a heap of red napkins with a reindeer design. 'It's lovely to see you here at last, Phillipa, but I'd better get back to work. These napkins won't fold themselves. Ben can drive you over to the house if you'd like to unpack.'

'I've come here to work,' Pippa told her firmly, 'and that's exactly what I shall do. I can unpack my case later. Just tell me what needs doing, and I'll get cracking.'

She was unconvinced by her great aunt's assurances that nothing was wrong. And as for this Cousin Ben, that was even more dubious. There was clearly something going on between the two of them, and she intended to discover exactly what it was. But now was not the right time. Perhaps later, up at the house, she might be able to get Aunty Evie alone …

'Well,' her great aunt said dubiously, 'I do need those three large boxes unpacked and the inventory checked.' She pointed to the storeroom, where cardboard boxes had been stacked untidily in the open doorway. 'If you're sure you're not too tired, dear?'

'Ben can help me,' she said tartly, stowing her handbag behind the counter and looking round at her cousin with raised eyebrows. 'Can't you, Ben?'

His eyes held hers a fraction longer than was comfortable. 'With pleasure, Pippa,' he murmured, indicating that she should precede him to the storeroom. 'With pleasure.'

It was very late that evening before Pippa, having helped prepare a warming Scottish supper of lamb chops with mashed potatoes and turnips, all smothered in a rich gravy, finally had a chance to be alone.

Her case unpacked, she flopped backwards onto her narrow single bed and stared up at the ceiling. It was not that the room was unappealing - apart from several stacks of ancient and obsolete Christmas-theme videos in one corner, taken off sale in the shop years ago, it was quite a cosy bedroom, with a quaint crocheted bed cover and purple fleece rug. But she no longer had the energy to remain in an upright position.

Tired as she was, it was hard not to keep remembering Ben at the dinner table, the sleeves of his crisp white shirt rolled to his elbows, watching her with an intensity that had left her skin prickling. She could see no family resemblance in him, not least because the men in her family were rarely that gorgeous. She adored her male relatives, of course, but she was not blind to the knowledge that they were more likely to resemble the turnip she had peeled for supper than the striking looks Ben had been blessed with.

But if he was *not* her cousin, why on earth had Aunt Evelyn claimed that he was? Had he fooled her in some diabolical way so he could worm his way into her affections and inherit her money?

No, it was impossible. Evelyn had her own little shop, it was true, and was not a poor woman, but she had no great fortune salted away that could tempt a criminal into a deception of that length. Besides, Ben did not seem like a man who made his living by befriending and scamming lonely pensioners. He looked far too dangerous for anything that small-time. And she was sure now that she had not imagined the flash of fear in her great aunt's eyes when Ben came into the shop tonight.

It seemed fantastical, but was her great aunt in some kind of trouble? If only she had been able to get her alone tonight. But Aunty Evie had seemed determined to avoid that, hurrying off to get ready for bed before Pippa could even ask her for a private chat.

Pippa heard noises from below. Doors opening and closing. Footsteps. Voices. Her great aunt turning in for the night, probably. Ben too, no doubt. It was only ten-thirty, but they all had an early start tomorrow.

Bedtime.

Slowly, painfully, she dragged herself up and reached for her night clothes, still folded from her suitcase and rather cool.

Shaking out the worst of the creases, she slipped into her loose pyjama trousers, shivering as she pulled the drawstring into a large bow. The snow might look lovely, but this kind of weather had its drawbacks. Especially in an old house with a dodgy heating system. She abandoned her warm socks with some misgiving, and hoped she would not need them in the night. Then, having unclipped her bra, she fastened her pyjama top buttons with cold fingers and slipped between the chilly sheets. Only then did she remember she had forgotten to take her knickers off.

'Oh well,' she muttered to herself. 'I'm not undressing again now.'

With the bedside lamp off, the room was oppressively dark for the first few minutes. She was used to streetlights and traffic noise in the London suburbs, and although this was not open countryside, it was still much quieter and darker than her bedroom at home.

Slowly her eyes began to adjust to the dark, until she could even make out through the curtains the dim on-off flash of some nearby Christmas lights. Suddenly she heard the high-pitched approach of police sirens, and stiffened. But they passed the house and died away. Finally her body started to relax.

'Who are you really, Ben Shakespeare?' she whispered, then closed her eyes, overcome with exhaustion.

Pippa was awakened some time later by a creaking on the landing outside her bedroom door, and jerked upwards with such a start that she almost knocked the bedside lamp off its wobbly little table.

At first she was confused, unaware of her surroundings. Then it came back to her. Scotland. Christmas. Great Aunt Evelyn. Ben Shakespeare.

He had been in her dream, she realised. There had been partial nudity involved, despite the cold weather. And some nibbling ...

How embarrassing!

Then the creaking came again. Still flushed and drowsy, she saw the thin strip of light under the door flicker, as though someone had just walked past. Yet the luminous hands of the bedside clock told her it was nearly three o'clock in the morning.

'Aunty Evie?' she whispered.

No answer.

Her great aunt's room was on the floor below, as was Ben's. The only other rooms on this floor were an ancient bathroom and a spare bedroom filled with dusty boxes and the accumulated bric-a-brac of over five decades, which was how long it had been since Evelyn had bought this house. To the best of her knowledge, there was no one else staying here.

So who on earth was outside her door?

She slipped out of bed in the darkness and was tiptoeing across the fleece rug when she suddenly realised her PJ bottoms were slowly and majestically descending her legs. It was an old but comfortable pair of pyjamas, and somehow the bow at her drawstring waist had come loose while she was sleeping.

Oh crikey! She clutched at them, bending to catch them before they hit her ankles, staggered forward a few steps with her bottom in the air, and tripped over some obstacle, unseen in the dark.

It was her empty suitcase, left with the lid thrown

back. She stepped into it, caught her pyjama-encumbered foot on the rim, and fell sideways into the stacks of old videos. The noise was tremendous. Like a rhino crashing through the percussion section of a orchestra.

She was lying facedown among the scattered videos, wondering if any of her bones could possibly be broken, when the door burst open and a piercingly bright spotlight hit her in the bottom.

Thank god she had not removed her underwear!

'What the hell?'

Heat flooded her face as she recognised that voice. Cousin Ben!

She groaned and turned over, knocking another stack of videos over in the process. He was a tall, dark figure silhouetted in the doorway, the landing light behind him, super-bright torch in his hand, shining it straight towards her. 'I ... fell,' she managed to say unnecessarily. Her arm came over her eyes as his torch dazzled her. 'Could you turn that light off, please?'

Ben hesitated, then snapped off the torch. The room was blessedly dark for a few seconds, then he clicked her main light on. 'What on earth were you doing?' he demanded, staring as she struggled to her feet. His voice sounded almost accusing. 'I thought you were being attacked.'

His eyes narrowed on her bare legs, and Pippa cringed, grabbing at her pyjama bottoms and hauling them back up. But not before she had noticed that she was wearing her Pussy knickers that day, of all the ones she could have chosen, big white pants with NICE PUSSY written across the rear.

Please God, she prayed fervently, let there be an earthquake right now. Anything to divert his attention from the most horribly embarrassing moment of her life ever.

'I was attacked,' she said tartly, knotting the waist drawstring twice over, so tight she would probably have to use scissors to release herself from it in the morning. 'By Christmas videos!'

He frowned at the scattered video cases, then turned his attention back to her, clearly unamused. 'But what were you doing out of bed?'

'I heard a noise. I was getting up to investigate when ... ' She hesitated, and her traitorous face blushed at the memory of her descending PJ bottoms.

One dark brow arched at her. 'Yes?'

'I tripped.' She kicked her suitcase. 'Over that.'

'I see,' he said drily.

Ben was fully dressed, she noticed with some bitterness. He was even still wearing his outdoor shoes. Then suspicion set in. 'Not asleep?' she asked, staring at his black jeans and sweater.

'I wasn't sleepy.'

She glanced at the clock. 'But it's gone three.'

He shrugged.

Definitely suspicious, she thought. 'So was it you? Making that noise outside my room?'

His dark, heavy-lidded eyes narrowed on her face again. It seemed to be one of his habitual expressions. Ben 'Squinty' Shakespeare, she thought spitefully, hoping that mocking her so-called cousin would make her feel less intimidated by him. But there was no ridding herself of the subtle undercurrent of awareness that started bubbling under her skin as soon as he was within ten feet of her. Gosh though, he was incredibly sexy. The infuriating bastard. Why couldn't he be balding and turnip-faced, like all the other cousins she had ever met? It simply wasn't fair. And if he was her cousin, distant or not, it felt very wrong to be eyeing him sideways like this.

'Yes, it was me. I couldn't find my phone.' He paused almost imperceptibly, as though making up a story on the fly. 'Evelyn sent me up to find something for her earlier, so I thought I might have left it in the spare room. Sorry if I disturbed you, creeping about.' He glanced at the fallen stacks of videos littering the floor. 'But at least Evelyn doesn't seem to have woken up.'

'Oh, Aunty Evie snores so loudly,' she said quickly, 'she wears earplugs to stop herself from waking up. She's all but deaf at night.'

'Good to know.'

She tried to study him secretly from under her eyelashes, which was remarkably difficult to do, she found, without looking like she had something in her eye. She did not trust him, not one little bit. But his explanation of the lost phone had sounded plausible. Except for that tiny hesitation. Her instincts were screaming at her to beware, and she always tried to credit her instincts with some sense where possible. Especially when it came to a stranger in her bedroom in the middle of the night.

Who was Ben and what was he hiding? More importantly, was Aunt Evelyn in danger with him in the house?

He certainly wasn't her cousin, as he had claimed, or even remotely Canadian. Unless she was just massively over-reacting to him and his brittle smile. If only she had managed to speak to Aunt Evelyn alone! But he seemed very careful to stop the two of them from ever being along together. Which was suspicious in itself.

Pippa crossed her arms and made a face like she was sucking a lemon, though with hindsight that probably wasn't very attractive. 'Do you do that often, then? Make phone calls in the middle of the night?'

'It isn't the middle of the night everywhere,' Ben remarked with the air of someone making a perfectly reasonable point, which he was. He slid his hands into his jeans pockets, watching her with the same intensity that had so disturbed her over supper. 'Anywhere, I wanted to set the alarm on my phone. Which was when I realised it was missing.'

Okay, that was definitely plausible. She often used the alarm on her own phone. There didn't seem to be much else to say. She made herself stop devouring him with her eyes like a sex-starved nun. Surely she had embarrassed herself enough for one night?

'Well, goodnight,' Pippa muttered, and tried to kick her annoying suitcase shut on her way back to the bed. The flimsy lid half shut, then fell back open again. Bloody hell.

Ben was smiling. 'Goodnight,' he said politely, and pulled the door shut as he left. 'Nice knickers, by the way.'

CHAPTER THREE

In Which Ben Pumps Santa (But Only After Pippa Blows Him First)

Her great aunt's Christmas Shop was in a block of other shops, squeezed between a newsagent's and a pet store, and easily one of the narrowest shops on the block. Her storage room, correspondingly, was like the inside of a glove. Hard to squeeze into, especially when stacked to the ceiling with open boxes spilling packaging and new stock, and hard to squeeze out of with anything in your arms broader than a box of Christmas tree baubles. The shop floor itself was only slightly wider, and cut into three distinct aisles by two five-foot-high display units, with the cash till tucked in behind the door. Each wall display was crammed with festive offerings of every kind, from illuminated outdoor decorations to the kind of fun or gimmicky trinkets and games that would fit into a child's Christmas stocking. All of which made most serious customers stop in their tracks and browse at a more leisurely pace, mini-basket in hand.

In other words, navigating the Christmas Shop during

opening hours was not easy. Especially now there were three members of staff permanently on duty, instead of the usual one or two.

For the first few days of working with Ben and Aunt Evelyn, it was not too bad. Ben was not too mocking, despite that inauspicious glimpse of her behind, and Pippa was determined not to spoil her great aunt's favourite time of year by being grumpy about this strange interloper.

But as the days passed, and the shopping frenzy deepened and became less entertaining, so her patience with Ben's highhanded ways began to crumble. So when Aunty Evie called her to the till two days before Christmas, while she was stretching to restock a high shelf with miniature reindeer figures, it took her considerable effort to squeeze past several uncooperative customers with heavy baskets, then down the next aisle where Ben had just unpacked a crate of flashing snowmen globes.

'Excuse me,' she stated loudly, but Ben did not move. 'I need to get past!'

'I'm stocking these shelves. Can't you just climb over me?' he asked, raising his eyebrows as though to insinuate that he had thought her more athletic than that.

Her jaw clenched, then she picked her way delicately over his body and the box of snow globes beside him. Only then did she realise why he had not moved. She was wearing a knee-length skirt with heels and warm winter tights, and he was admiring her legs as she climbed past.

His smile made her want to bash him with one of the snow globes, but she restrained herself with amazing self-control.

'Sorry,' she said, finally reaching the counter to find her aunt deep in conversation with a harassed-looking man in his early thirties. 'You need me, Aunty Evie?'

'Och, there you are, Pippa!' her great aunt exclaimed, and held out a long slim cardboard box with a Santa figure on it. 'This gentlemen is in a tearing hurry. He and his wife are hosting a Christmas party in an hour for his little girl and her classmates. Thirty-two five-year-olds! And I sold him an inflatable Santa for his party last week, only the damn thing won't stay inflated.' She waved a bumpy, fat shred of red and black plastic at her. 'I've had a look, and there's a big tear right by the air hole. So I'm giving him another one free of charge. Could you inflate it for him? Or it won't be ready in time for the party.'

She held the box, staring at her great aunt. '*Inflate it?*'

'Aye, dear, could you? It's not difficult, there's a pump in the storage room. Shouldn't take more than ten minutes.' Her great aunt frowned when Pippa did not immediately move. 'Come on, Pippa. Be a sport, dear. Think of all those five year olds.'

'Of course.' Pippa smiled reluctantly at the man, who did not smile back. Miserable sod. Though the prospect of spending several hours in a room packed with hordes of five-year-olds would make most sane people miserable, she conceded. 'One inflated Santa coming right up.'

Ben smiled maliciously up at her as she stepped over him in aisle two. 'I would help,' he assured her mendaciously, 'only I must get all these snow globes unpacked before closing time.'

She said nothing, merely narrowed her eyes at him. To her relief, he had never mentioned the first night incident in her bedroom again. But his embarrassing 'nice knickers' remark was still at the forefront of her mind, as was the memory of her bottom in the glare of his torch beam. Hard to shake that image, really.

In the store room, she dragged the plastic Santa out of its pack and gazed down at the instructions in consternation. LIFESIZE INFLATABLE SANTA.

'Lifesize?' she repeated in a hollow voice.

She put down the Santa and searched the room for the mythical pump, turning over most of the boxes in her hunt. There was no sign of a pump. She considered going back to ask Aunt Evie where exactly it was, but then remembered Ben. His mocking smile was not something she wished to provoke again.

She knelt, unfolded the Santa figure, and searched for the air valve. To her horror it was situated in the worst possible place, right at the base of Santa's bottom. Almost between his legs.

'Fantastic.'

She pulled the air valve straight, bent over almost to the floor, and gave a few experimental puffs.

His groin twitched in a disconcerting manner.

'Bloody hell.'

She bent again and blew more air into the valve. She blew until she was red in the face. Santa's nether regions began to swell. Very, very slowly.

Pippa sat back and glared at his skinny red backside. No way this was going to take ten minutes! But there was no point complaining, not unless she wanted Ben to think she wasn't up to the job.

If she could only find the pump ...

But of course she couldn't. Giving up the fruitless search, she bent again to blow more air into the inflatable Santa, pleased to see him beginning to swell and grow after another few minutes. Perhaps it would not take as long as she had thought. Though the ominous word 'lifesize' kept echoing in her head as she blew and blew, feeling a little lightheaded after a while. This must be what hyperventilating is like, she thought.

She held up the Santa, holding her finger firmly over the air valve. Both legs were now almost fully inflated, and most of his chest, but his head and arms were still shrivelled in comparison. He looked like a mutant Santa with a white goatee, she thought, his withered smile seeming to accuse her of not making enough of an effort.

How much larger would he grow, she wondered, eyeing his stout legs and belly dubiously? And how much bloody longer would it take to fully inflate him?

'Come on,' Pippa told herself impatiently. 'You can't let yourself be defeated by an inflatable man!'

Knees aching on the hard floor of the store room, she bent again to her task, the swelling Santa beginning to eclipse her head as she puffed and panted, rather like a huge red balloon with a black belt round its increasingly rotund waist.

Puff. Puff. Puff.

Head bent to her seemingly endless task, she suddenly became aware of a draught.

Pippa looked up from between large red plastic thighs to see the store room door open and Ben in the doorway, staring down at her with a bemused expression.

Utterly aghast, Pippa felt the kind of embarrassment normally reserved for leaving the loo with your skirt tucked in your knickers or unknowingly smiling at people with spinach in your teeth.

Her cheeks flooded with heat and she could only stare back at him in horror, mouth still pursed like a goldfish's, mid-blow.

'Pippa, what on earth are you doing to that Santa?' he demanded, not unreasonably.

'B… blowing him …' she managed to gasp, '*up.* Obviously!'

'You were supposed to use the pump.' His dark eyebrows had flexed so high they looked like railway bridge arches. 'We're getting ready to close. You've been in here for ages. That customer is still waiting though. He's going to be late for his daughter's party.'

Behind him she could see the harassed-looking customer also peering into the store room, eyes widening at the sight of the sales assistant on her knees, giving mouth-to-bottom to his inflatable Santa.

'I … I couldn't find the pump.' Struggling to get her breath back, she held the semi-inflated Santa out to him. 'Here, that's the best I could do,' she said, then added defensively, 'His head's … almost done.'

Ben took the limp Santa from her and examined his shrunken head with an unreadable expression. 'So I see.'

To her amazement, he tucked the Santa effortlessly under one arm, reached up to the third shelf without even looking away from her, and brought down a pump. This he spun like a gunslinger, inserting its working-end into Santa's bottom-hole, and began to pump hard with his free arm.

Santa grew like a mad soufflé until his fat head bulged, white beard fully extended, belly losing all its little wrinkles and bumps. Less than a minute later he was indeed 'lifesize'.

Ben extracted the pump and handed him out to the waiting customer with an apologetic smile. 'There you go, sir,' he said smoothly. 'Sorry about the delay. He's all yours.'

The telephone was ringing as the customer, grim-faced, strode away with his replacement Santa.

The store room door swung shut as Ben turned back, shutting them in together. She could find nothing to say, acutely aware of his proximity in the narrow space. He replaced the pump on the high shelf, then turned to her, the ghost of a smile hovering on his lips.

Ben had not actually laughed at her, she realised with sudden gratitude. But she could see the mockery in his face.

'Need any help getting up?' He held out a hand, his eyes locked on hers. 'Though you do look rather fetching on your knees.'

Her hair had worked loose from her ponytail, she realised, tucking the wayward strands behind her ear with a cross expression. Cross and humiliated. And maybe a little flushed as well. Because she knew *precisely* what he was thinking.

'Thank you,' she muttered, and let him pull her to her feet.

Suddenly they were chest to chest in the cramped space, face to face, and oh my goodness, his eyes were so attractive …

His smile faded as he studied her, and his face grew serious. 'Pippa,' he began softly, but never got any further.

'Ben? Ben?'

His head turned sharply. It was her great aunt calling him in a querulous, high-pitched voice. Pippa thought she had never heard her sound so afraid.

Before she knew what was happening, Ben was through the store room door and gone. Taken aback by the speed of his reaction, she followed quickly. There had been a note in Evelyn's voice that left her cold with fear. What could be wrong?

Her great aunt was standing by the till, leaning on the counter, holding the telephone in her hand. Her face was pale, her eyes wide. 'It was him,' she said hoarsely. 'I … I didn't say anything. But he said my name. *My name!*'

Ben sounded surprisingly calm. Cool, even. 'It's okay, Evelyn, everything's going to be okay.'

'But he knew it was me. He knows where I am!'

He took the telephone from her unresisting hand, pressed the menu button and glanced at the screen. 'Number withheld.'

Her great aunt looked terrified. 'We've got to get out of here. And Pippa too. Oh my god. He'll kill us all.'

That was too much for Pippa. This situation had gone beyond vague suspicions now and was starting to sound downright dangerous.

'*Kill us?*' She looked from one to the other, confused and disturbed, and folded her arms tightly across her chest. 'Right, what the hell is going on here? Aunty Evie, what's this all about? And please don't tell me it's not my business. Because I can see that you are *very* frightened, and I need to know the truth now.'

Ben did not even look at her. 'Not yet. There isn't time. Your aunt's right. We have to leave here at once.'

He gave a cursory look up and down the aisles. 'Good, no customers left. Pippa, get the lights, would you? And Evelyn, lock and bolt the door. I'll go out the back way and bring the car round to the fire exit.'

'Now wait a minute – ' Pippa began hotly, but he did not let her finish.

'No time,' Ben told her crisply, collecting the car keys from the hook behind the counter. 'If you value your aunt's life, just do what you've been asked.'

And with that he was gone. It seemed one second he was there, the next the metal back door was banging shut behind him.

Pippa did not move at first, her arms still folded, every muscle tensed with frustration. She wanted answers and was determined not to be brushed aside again. Especially by a man she hardly knew and did not even particularly like. Even if he was pretty hot.

But when Evelyn stumbled towards the door with her keys, dropping them twice on the way, she suddenly caught the sense of urgency.

'Here, give me those, Aunty Evie,' she insisted, chiding her great aunt as she took charge of the keys. 'You shouldn't be walking about on that bad ankle. Let me lock the door, for goodness' sake. You sit down and wait for Ben to come back.'

But as she was fitting the key into the lock, a sudden rustle behind her in the tinsel and wrapping paper aisle made them both jump.

She spun round to find a little old lady standing there, holding up a large rubber reindeer. 'I'm sorry,' the lady squeaked in a strong Scottish accent, looking more than a little confused, 'I'm sure I didn't mean to outstay my welcome. Is the store shutting early? I just want this for my mantelpiece.'

Her heart thumping violently, Pippa sagged in relief against the door. For a second there she had half-expected to see a murderer with a gun or a knife emerging from the tinsel aisle.

'Yes,' she managed to gasp, 'yes, we're shutting early.' She jerked the door open and snowflakes whirled in icily.

Great, she thought. The snow had started falling again. Just what they needed. 'You'd better go, madam, before we shut you in for the night.'

The old lady bent to fumble in her tartan shopping trolley for her purse. Her crocheted blue hat looked like a tea cosy. 'Aye, aye. How much for the reindeer first?'

'Take it!' Evelyn exclaimed, hobbling up behind the lady and pushing her out of the half-open door. 'It's free!'

The lady seemed astonished, clutching the rubber reindeer to her chest as she tripped over the step into the snowy street. 'But ... Well, that's very kind of you.' She smiled weakly up at them. 'Any chance I could take two, then? A matching pair, like?'

'Sorry.' Pippa thrust her shopping trolley after her, then shut the door in her face.

The door having been locked and bolted, she hit the lights.

The shop was plunged into darkness, the gloomy interior lit only by the constant on-off flash of Evelyn's Christmas window decorations. Green and blue lights chased each other round the window frame every few seconds, the illuminated reindeer noses glowing an eerie red under draped tinsel.

'There,' she said with grim satisfaction, then turned to look at Evelyn's guilty expression. 'Now, Aunty Evie, maybe you can tell me what all this is about. Ben isn't really my cousin, is he?'

Aunt Evelyn bit her lip, then shook her head. 'No, dear. He's not.'

'Who is he, then?'

'He's a policeman,' she whispered, as though afraid there were more little old ladies hiding among the tinsel-covered aisles.

Pippa stared, thoroughly bemused. 'A *policeman?*'

'I'm afraid so.'

'So I was right, Aunty Evie. You *are* in trouble.'

'Aye,' she agreed miserably, still whispering. 'I am

that.'

Pippa found herself whispering too, almost by instinct. 'What ... what kind of trouble?'

Aunt Evelyn shook her head, twisting her hands in anguish. 'Oh drugs, of course. What else?'

'Drugs?' Pippa felt like she was going mad. Her great aunt had always seemed so sweet and law-abiding. What on earth had she got herself mixed up in? 'But, Aunty Evie, you ... you don't take drugs. The strongest thing I've ever seen you take was an extra-strength aspirin.'

'Not me, them. The men who are after me.'

Okay, now she was going mad. 'I'm sorry? Which men? And why are they after you?'

'The men who want to kill me. They're the ones with the drugs. The head man, he's a duke or something. Very important man.' She waved her hand vaguely. 'It was like I told you before, except some of it was a fib. I did go to Glasgow, visiting my brother Gregory. And for a spot of shopping too. They have such fine stores there.'

Pippa nodded encouragingly.

'Well, it was very late when I got back to my hotel, and I'd had a wee bit too much food. Och, it was a very tasty spread my brother laid on for me. But very filling, so I had to walk it off before I could go to bed. You understand?'

'Mmm,' Pippa managed, still trying to figure out what role a 'duke' could have played in all this.

'So I took a walk around the block. And I was just passing this alley behind the hotel when I heard ... rat-a-tat-tat!'

Pippa stared. 'Rat-a-tat-tat?'

Her aunt, very white-faced, made an odd gesture like someone shaking a colander to strain peas, then whispered hoarsely, 'Gunfire!'

'Oh!' Pippa's mouth opened wide. '*Rat-a-tat-tat!*'

'Like in The Godfather.'

'Yes! Yes!'

Aunt Evelyn shook the colander again. Only more violently, and side to side. '*Rat-a-tat-tat*! And down they all fell.'

'Who?'

'The two men, the … victims. Whoever they were.' Her aunt put a hand to her face, remembering. 'And I shrieked. Stupid, really. I should just have kept walking. But I stood there and shrieked. And the man, the duke, he turned and looked straight at me.' She shook her head in consternation, really frightened now. It was in her eyes. '*Straight at me!*'

'Oh my god.'

'So I set off running, fast as I could, which wasn't very fast, and I slipped over on the icy pavement. That's how I hurt my ankle. Well, I ducked into the side entrance of the hotel. I heard someone run past, but I just kept going. All I could think was getting back to my room. I got to the lift, pressed the button, waited. Then I looked round, and there was one of the men in the hotel lobby, staring at me.'

Pippa could hardly breathe. 'Did he hurt you?'

'Och, no.' Her aunt made a tutting noise under her breath. 'We were in public. But he pulled out his phone.'

'And took a photo of you on it?'

'Aye, that he did,' Evelyn agreed grimly. 'So when I rang the police, and described the other man, this duke, they said I was in danger. But I still want to testify against him. Nasty murdering man.'

'I don't understand. He's a duke?'

Aunt Evelyn nodded impatiently. 'One of these gangsters who's big into drugs.'

Suddenly she understood. 'You mean a drug *baron*!'

'Baron, aye, that's the one. I always get it wrong. Anyway, they sent me home with Ben to look after me until the trial, just in case the drug baron found out where I lived and sent his men to … well, to shut me up.' Her great aunt looked contrite and a little tearful. 'And now you're in danger too, Phillipa. I wanted to warn you not to come up this year, but Ben said I shouldn't do anything out of the ordinary. Nothing to draw attention to myself.'

'I'm glad I'm here, Aunty Evie,' Pippa reassured her, and gave her a quick hug. 'You're shaking! We must get you out of here. Where on earth's Ben with the car?'

At that moment, someone tried to open the shop door. Not hard, but the frame rattled. Behind the door, which was decorated with dancing Santas and elves, they could see the dark figure of a man.

Aunt Evelyn gave a frightened cry, and Pippa hushed her. They stood in silence, staring at the door in the flashing neon darkness, about three feet away.

The metal flap of the letterbox lifted and a large, hairy hand appeared beneath it. Its fingers crept around the rim of the flap, feeling their way slowly; one of the fingers had a thick gold ring on it, another was crooked, as though it had been broken in the past and mended badly.

'Open this door!' the man on the other side insisted hoarsely, bending to speak through the letterbox.

He had a thick Scottish accent, and an unpleasant edge to his voice. Suddenly Pippa was reminded of the man outside the shop when she arrived, the huge man walking the Pekinese. He had been wearing a gold ring too.

'Open this door or we'll break it down. We know you're in there. There's no point hiding, Evelyn.'

CHAPTER FOUR

Of Pine Cones, Candy Canes, and Handguns

Pippa grabbed the nearest large object – it happened to be a giant edible red and white striped candy cane, about four foot long and still wrapped in plastic – and rapped the man's fingers with it.

The hand was jerked back, accompanied by a yelp of pain. 'Bitch!' he swore, then thrust his hand back through, groping about as though trying to grab her.

Aunt Evelyn's face stiffened at that. 'Well … !'

She relieved Pippa of her giant candy cane with a muttered, 'Excuse me, dear,' then smacked it sharply down across the back of his wandering hand. 'Watch your language!'

The candy cane cracked audibly; its crook hung down limply as Evelyn retracted it. 'Oh dear,' she said miserably, trying to fix it and failing. She threw it aside with a clatter. 'That one's a goner.'

The man had howled at his punishment, withdrawing his hand again in a hurry. There was some shouting in such a thick accent that Pippa could not follow it, but she knew swear words when she heard them. Seconds later, the door shook in its frame as he started to thump into it with his shoulder. 'You wait till I get in there. I'll make you suffer for that, old woman!'

Furious that anyone could threaten her great aunt, Pippa grabbed two more giant candy canes and banged on the door, shouting, 'Go away! We've called the police, you know.'

Suddenly the emergency exit at the back of the shop was thrown open.

Someone stumbled inside, knocking a Christmas card spinner to the floor with a crash. Snow whirled in with the newcomer, tiny dancing points of white in the darkness blinding her.

Another man!

Startled, Pippa dropped the candy canes and looked about for a better weapon. In sudden inspiration, she seized a vast gold-sprayed pine cone from the traditional Scottish decorations display and lobbed it at the dark figure in the doorway.

'Ouch, bloody hell!' he exclaimed, staggering forward into the neon flash from the shop window, and Pippa bit her lip as his face was lit up.

'Sorry, Ben!'

'Yes, so am I. What in God's name *was* that?'

'A super-large pine cone sprayed with gold paint. £3.99 or £9.99 for three.'

He was rubbing his forehead, glaring at her. 'This is precisely why I hate Christmas. Good shot though.'

'Thanks, I was on the netball team at school. But I thought you were one of *them*.'

'*Them?*'

Pippa pointed at the door, where the man could still be heard thumping and muttering. The safety glass had cracked now, under several well-aimed kicks. She dropped her voice to a conspiratorial whisper. 'There's at least one out there. Maybe more. A Bad Man. He tried to stick his hand through the letterbox, but we hit him with a candy cane. Several candy canes, in fact.'

'Mine broke,' Aunt Evelyn added sourly.

Ben's mouth twisted, but he did not comment. Instead he reached – and none too gently – for Evelyn's arm. 'Come on, both of you. Sounds like he's planning to do some late night Christmas shopping, and it would be better if we weren't here by the time he gets in. I've got the car at the back. The engine's running.'

'But my shop … It's all I've got, Ben,' Aunt Evelyn exclaimed, 'and I'll be damned if I'm going to let a bunch of *Glaswegians* wreck it!'

Aunt Evelyn resisted him, her face a little wild and flushed. With a mutinous expression, she grabbed onto a gold-winged fairy dangling on a wire from the ceiling as though hoping this would tether her to the place. 'No, no! I have to defend my stock. Elves to the rescue! Man the battlements!'

'They're not after your stock, Evelyn,' he reminded her grimly. 'They're here to kill you. Now let go of that fairy.'

It was dark and cold in the alley behind the shop, snow biting their faces and bare hands. Pippa and Ben helped the hobbling Evelyn into the back of the car. Pippa bundled in beside her, then Ben drove off at speed.

'Oh goodness, stop!' Evelyn exclaimed, struggling to find her seat belt in the dark. 'I'm not ready, I haven't got my seat belt on! What if you have to brake suddenly?'

'Help her,' Ben threw over his shoulder at Pippa.

Please, she thought darkly, but helped Evelyn locate her seat belt and plug it in. Hurriedly she put on her own belt, swaying back and forth as Ben cornered far too fast before accelerating up the snowy hill. She thought of the man back at the shop, and wondered how dangerous he was.

Had that man really come there to kill her great aunt? It seemed almost incredible

'So you're a policeman?' she asked, staring at his dark profile. 'Not my cousin?'

'Evelyn told you the truth? Yes, I'm a police offer. Undercover. Sorry about the "cousin" cover story, we couldn't risk you being suspicious about why I was there and talking about it on social media.'

'Talking about … ' Her mouth opened, then shut again in dismay. 'I can't even get a signal on my phone, actually. So Twitter is right out, for a start. Not that I'm a social media junkie!'

'No?' He sounded unapologetic. 'Your aunt said you were always on Facebook.'

She turned to remonstrate with Aunt Evelyn, then saw how frightened she was looking. 'Now don't worry,' she reassured her, though she was feeling far from happy herself. 'Everything's going to be fine. Ben will get you home safe, then he'll call his colleagues and – '

But he was slowing down as they approached Evelyn's house, frowning at the road ahead. 'That doesn't look good.'

There was a black van parked outside the big old Victorian house, lit up in the headlights. Outside on the pavement, three rugged-looking men in dark coats were gathered around the gleam of what appeared to be a smartphone screen, heads bent as though studying something or listening to a call on speaker phone.

Ben drove past without stopping.

'Wait, wait, you've missed the house,' Evelyn told him, sounding bewildered. 'It's back there.'

'We're not going to the house,' he replied shortly.

'Those men … ' Pippa looked back through the rear window, making sure no one was following them. 'Were they after Aunty Evie too?'

'I should imagine so.'

'Oh no, they're not at my house too, are they?' Her great aunt shrunk back into the seat, her face drawn with misery. 'But what's going to happen to poor Nicholas? If those vile men get their brutish hands on him ...'

Pippa looked at her in consternation. She had not been aware of anyone else living in the house this week. 'Who's Nicholas?'

'Her goldfish,' Ben said drily.

Evelyn sounded on the verge of tears. 'He's a Koi, not a goldfish. I keep him in the ornamental pond in the back garden. I've only had him a year, but we were just starting to get along. I named him Nicholas after Santa's real name in legend. You know, *Saint Nicholas.*' She managed a smile when Pippa patted her cold hands. 'I should have introduced you two before now, but it's all been such a rush with Christmas coming and the shop ... Nicholas has such a jolly red belly though, and a pure white chin. Just like his namesake.'

'I'm sure he'll be fine, Aunty Evie.'

Ben drove for a while without speaking, his eyes watching the road ahead and behind, constantly flicking to the mirror. But there was no sign of headlights. Soon they were heading out of town on the road that ran alongside the railway line.

Pippa sat forward, speaking quietly so Aunt Evelyn would not hear. 'How dangerous are these men? Surely they don't plan to *kill* my great aunt? It seems insane.'

'I'm afraid it's only too likely.' His face was tight. 'I was asked to stay here with her, keep an eye out for anything suspicious until the trial date came up. I didn't believe they would track her down so easily, not all the way out here. The man she identified is in custody, of course, but his friends will stop at nothing to prevent her from testifying.'

'So it really is that serious?'

He nodded, glancing in the rear view mirror, then muttered, 'Sit back. I need to do something.'

Glancing behind them, she saw headlights following. Suddenly Ben spun off the main road without warning, taking a narrow lane between high fences, and she realised it was the town industrial estate.

He snapped out the lights and for a moment they were driving unseen, navigating by the infrequent streetlamps through the estate.

Ben accelerated off the road and through two solid metal gates marked PRIVATE. He stopped the car, jumped out and pushed the doors shut behind them. Then he got back in and drove slowly through the darkness until they reached the glimmering outline of an unlit building with TYRES, SPARES & REPAIRS painted in faded blue lettering on the side.

He turned off the engine, then glanced back at her and Aunt Evelyn. 'Stay here,' he said grimly. 'Don't make a sound. And whatever you do, don't try to make a phone call.'

'Who would I call?' she muttered after he had shut the door and left, watching his dark figure disappear round the other side of the building, presumably in search of a door. 'Ghostbusters?'

Her great aunt was looking very pale and cold. Pippa rubbed her hands to warm them up. 'Hey, how are you bearing up?'

But all Evelyn could do was shake her head and make a quiet moaning noise. She was clearly very distressed.

'Ben will look after us,' Pippa said reassuringly, then froze at the sound of an engine nearby.

'What's that?' Aunt Evelyn exclaimed, and Pippa held up a hand.

'Shh, not a sound, remember?' She peered out through the whirling snow flakes obscuring the windscreen, and saw headlights slowly passing along the road to their left.

'Is it them?' her aunt whispered.

'I don't know. Perhaps,' she said, but she could see now that it was a large black van. Just like the one that had been parked outside the house.

Any second now the van would drive straight past

their hiding place. Luckily the yard they were in had a solid metal fence and gate, so they were unlikely to be visible from the road.

But if the men should decide to get out of their van and come back with a torch …

Ben appeared at the back door, opening it silently. Without speaking he gestured them both to get out, a finger across his lips, then helped Aunt Evelyn out of the car. It was freezing, snow underfoot and gently falling, and neither of them had their coats. But it was better to be a bit cold than dead, Pippa considered.

He led them to the back of the building and through an open side door. 'In there and up the stairs,' he said quietly, pointing the way to Pippa. 'Sorry, but you'll have to manage the stairs in the dark. No lights allowed.'

'I think they just drove past,' she told him urgently.

'I saw them,' he agreed, and then shocked her by pulling a small black handgun from inside his jacket and checking it. 'As soon as it's safe, I'll move the car under cover. They may recognise it otherwise.'

Her breath had caught in her throat. 'Is that a … You've got *a gun?*'

His smile mocked her. 'What, did you expect me to beat them off with a candy cane?'

'Oh my god.'

'Look after your aunt. I won't be long.' He pushed her inside the building after her great aunt, and disappeared again.

Pippa turned back to Aunt Evelyn, her eyes trying to become accustomed to the darkness, and was horrified to see her shambling figure already hopping up the metal stairs to the first floor.

'Aunty Evie, stop!' she hissed.

But her great aunt merely beckoned her to follow. 'Come on, it's up here. He said upstairs, didn't he?'

'Shh!'

Pippa hurried after her, tripping over several

obstacles in the darkness, still reeling from the shock of seeing Ben with a handgun. Somehow that made everything real. She also fervently hoped that he really was a policeman, and they had not just let themselves be abducted by a man who was clearly armed and dangerous.

She tried not to remember his wicked smile. *What, did you expect me to beat them off with a candy cane?*

Oh, he really was scrumptious. And the kind of man any sensible woman should keep firmly at arms' length. Because after nearly a week living and working in close proximity, even with her great aunt as a gooseberry in the background, that smile was too knowing. He *knew* she fancied him. Worse still, he knew *she knew* he knew she fancied him. Which was far too much knowing for anyone's good. And probably in a thoroughly Biblical sense, she thought darkly.

At the top of the stairs was a small room. The door was ajar, and she saw a glimmer of light from inside. Hurrying inside, she shut the door. 'Aunty Evie, Ben said no lights!'

'But there aren't any windows,' her great aunt pointed out, reasonably enough. 'What harm can it do? Besides, he can't expect us to sit around in the dark for hours.'

Sure enough, the small room had no windows, and the only light was a small table lamp. It illuminated a table covered in electrical equipment, several chairs, a battered old sofa with a blanket across it, and a kettle area with a sink.

'Home Sweet Home,' Pippa muttered, and watched her aunt hobble to the sink and fill the kettle.

'This is turning into quite an adventure,' Aunt Evelyn said cheerfully, humming under her breath as she poked around beside the kettle. Then she bent to rummage under the sink, emerging with some cheap mugs. 'Tea or coffee, dear? I think they've got both. Though only powdered milk, I'm afraid.'

'Aunty Evie, are you sure about Ben?' Pippa asked

urgently, leaning back against the door. 'I mean, he is definitely one of the good guys? Not a ... a gangster?'

'Oh yes, dear,' Evelyn said comfortably, wiping the cups with a filthy-looking dishcloth. 'I'm no fool. I took a peep at his credentials when he thought I wasn't looking.'

'*What?*'

'He was in the bath. And I ... peeked.'

'Aunty Evie!'

Her aunt turned, seeing her horrified expression, then looked shocked. 'Oh, not *those* credentials!' She giggled suddenly, hiding her face in the dishcloth. 'Goodness me, Ben's young enough to be my grandson. No, I mean while he was in the bathroom, I went through the pockets of his jacket and trousers. Found his wallet, and his ID.'

'Right, I thought you meant ... '

'Though I did catch a glimpse of his bottom once,' Aunt Evelyn added conspiratorially. 'When he was getting dressed and left his bedroom door open a crack. Oh, it was very nice.' She sighed, and clasped the dishcloth to her narrow chest. 'A very nice bottom indeed.'

'Aunty Evie!'

'Sorry, dear. But getting older doesn't mean you don't notice young men.' Her aunt winked at her. 'It's just you learn to pretend you *haven't* noticed.'

'Perhaps you could learn not to mention that you had noticed, as well.' Pippa left the door, breathing more easily. She was trying not to think of her great aunt spying on Ben in the nude. Though she wouldn't mind a glimpse of his rather tight-looking bottom herself ...

'But at least Ben is who he says he is,' she added, and managed a crooked smile. 'That's a weight off my mind.'

A dry voice in the doorway behind her said, 'What's a weight off your mind?' and she turned, blushing hotly at the thought that Ben might have heard them talking about his naked bottom.

'N ... nothing,' she stammered, trying to turn back to him too quickly and tripping over a wire instead. With her usual grace, she pitched face-first onto the sofa, then bounced off onto the hard floor. 'Ouch!'

Ben was there in an instant, of course. He held out a hand, bending over her. 'Need some help?' he asked with an edge of irony, and she could see that he was remembering that first night, and her knickers …

He straightened up with her in his arms, and she tried not to meet his gaze. 'Better?' he asked.

'I'm fine.'

'You seem to make a habit of falling over.'

Her lips tightened. She knew he hadn't forgotten! 'You can let go now,' she told him icily.

He released her with a shrug.

'So where are we?' she demanded. 'I thought you would have taken us to a police station. Somewhere safe. Not this … ' She glanced about at the grim little room, lost for words.

'Hole?' he suggested.

'Well, it's cold and not very comfortable,' she pointed out defensively. 'And how safe is it? Those men are probably out there right now, looking for us.'

He nodded, sinking his hands into his jeans pockets. 'I think we gave them the slip, and the car's out of sight now. But yes, it's not one hundred percent safe here. But there isn't a police station anywhere for miles. Not one that's manned round the clock, anyway, or prepared for a possible shoot-out with those men.'

She turned and stared at Aunt Evelyn. 'Is that true?'

'Cuts, dear,' Evelyn agreed sadly. 'Government cuts. They've closed so many of our little rural stations. And we'd probably have to drive several hours to the nearest one that's open at night.'

'So we hide?' she asked him, horrified. 'That's the plan?'

'This is a safe house,' he said shortly, and turned to lock the door, then pocketed the key. 'I set it up a few weeks back, just in case this kind of scenario happened.

Though I hoped it wouldn't be needed. There's no mobile phone signal here, unfortunately. But I had a landline installed, so I can still ring for back-up. Meanwhile we stay put.'

She watched in disbelief as he picked up the phone and started punching out a number. 'For how long?'

'Until my back-up arrives.'

Aunt Evelyn was fidgeting as the kettle started to boil. 'Ben, is there a … a convenience here? A ladies' room?'

'Through there,' he said, nodding towards one of two narrow doorways that led off the room.

She disappeared apologetically, leaving Pippa to make the tea. She did so automatically, stirring powdered milk into the steaming mugs of coffee and watching it dissolve as she listened to Ben's brief, muttered phone conversation.

He rang off, frowning. 'They don't think anyone can get out to us for three or four hours. Maybe longer.'

'*What?*'

'I was afraid this might happen,' he admitted. 'But it can't be helped. There are some biscuits under the sink, and plenty of coffee. It's cold, but we should be able to hole up here until dawn without too much hardship.'

Aunt Evelyn reappeared, looking a bit less fraught than before. She had tidied her wild hair too, and to Pippa's relief looked much less frail than before.

'What's up, laddy?' she asked Ben at once, seeing his expression. 'No cavalry coming?'

'Sorry, Evelyn. It seems there's been a serious situation to the west of us, and the guys who would have scrambled are already attending there. The best they can do at short notice is to send a small team up from Glasgow. But of course everyone's gone home for the night, so it's going to take time to get them all in and briefed. Then they have to get here. Though my boss says he'll see about getting permission to use one of the police helicopters.'

Pippa was outraged. 'But … we could be killed!'

'No,' he said smoothly, 'it's not as bad as that. We're safe enough until the morning. I'm fairly certain those men didn't see us come in here. Otherwise I would have insisted on an emergency response.'

'But can't one of the local police … ?'

He looked at Pippa drily. 'You want to put a local copper up against those men? We need special officers trained in firearms and precisely this kind of gang confrontation. No, this is the best way for everyone. Coffee, a few hours' sleep, and you'll both be free. Nothing to worry about.'

She was not convinced. And when he took out his handgun a few minutes later, laying it on the table beside his coffee mug, she felt even less comfortable.

Aunt Evelyn was soon yawning though, despite the coffee, which she put aside only half-finished. Pippa was not surprised; the powdered milk tasted like out-of-date talcum powder.

'Well, I've had enough excitement today to last me a year or ten.' Her great aunt stretched, and a button popped on her dress. 'Oops!' She dragged her cardigan shut to hide the gap. 'Did you mention sleep, Ben? I take it there's a bed somewhere in this place?'

Ben pointed to the other doorway. 'Only one bed, I'm afraid. And it's a single, fold-up bed.'

'I can sleep on the floor,' Pippa said stoutly.

'Not enough room in there,' he told her, and nodded to the unappealing sofa. 'That's your best bet. I wasn't expecting to house two people, I'm afraid.'

Aunt Evelyn kissed her on the cheek and slipped away into the other room, still yawning. 'Night, all,' she muttered vaguely, closing the door behind her.

'So where are you going to sleep?' Pippa asked him, frowning down at the battered sofa with its sad little blanket. The temperature had already dropped since they came inside, and she could guess it was going to be a long, cold night.

'I'm not going to sleep,' Ben said succinctly, and sat back on one of the plastic chairs right opposite the sofa. He put his feet up on the table and crossed them comfortably, the handgun always just within reach. His eyes met hers steadily. 'I'm going to watch.'

Pervert, she thought, looking back at him through squinty eyes. But she said nothing.

Instead she visited the toilet herself, which had a small oval mirror on the wall, did the necessary, then washed her hands and face, and tidied her hair. She had left her handbag behind at the shop, so there was no chance of patching up her make-up. But he would only have guffawed at her if she had put lipstick and foundation on to go to bed, she reminded herself. Better to look pale and interesting than tarty, anyway.

Then she strolled back out and tried to make herself comfortable too, lying down on the sofa and dragging the blanket over her head.

'Goodnight,' she said, her voice muffled by the blanket.

'Goodnight,' he replied, but she heard the ghost of laughter in his voice as she turned over, burying her head in the lone cushion the sofa had to offer.

It was almost as if he knew what she was thinking. A night in a safe house, being protected from a gang of hardened criminals ... and her pulse was racing out of excitement, not fear.

CHAPTER FIVE

On Getting Stuffed

So it was not the most promising night's sleep ever. It turned out the blanket was scratchy and smelt suspiciously of fish, and most of the sofa's springs were broken. And eager to come out and make that point themselves. Again and again. Mostly in her bottom region.

She discovered this last fact about an hour later when, turning over in an uneasy doze vaguely resembling sleep, a spring attacked her bum. Sharply and with venom.

'Ouch!' she exclaimed, and jerked up.

Ben was reading some papers at the table. He got up and came over, a look of amusement on his face. 'Problem?'

'Something just poked me in the ... These bloody springs are broken!'

'Sorry about that. It was the best I could get at short notice and without drawing attention to this place.'

'Yes, well, I suppose it's not your fault.' She rubbed surreptitiously at her sore bottom, then swung her legs off the sofa and stood up. Her chin felt damp – had she been drooling in her sleep? she wondered in horror, quickly running a hand across her lips – and her hair was probably doing one of its nesting swallows' impersonation, by the look on his face. 'But I don't think I'll be able to get any more sleep. Not on that thing.'

He surveyed her dispassionately, then went back to fetch her a tissue from a box on the table.

'Thank you,' she said in awful tones, and turned away to dry her face. So she had been drooling. Bloody, bloody, bloody.

'Couldn't sleep, eh?' he murmured, taking the used tissue from her, rolling it up and chucking it with uncanny accuracy into the wastepaper bin. 'Well, maybe I should find something to keep us amused while you're awake, then.'

'If you're going to suggest charades,' she began hotly, then was silenced when he drew her into his arms and kissed her.

Abandoning all pretence that she did not want him to kiss her, Pippa ran her hands into his short dark hair and pulled him close. 'Mmm,' she said as he lifted his head to look down at her.

A languorous smile curved his lips. 'Like that, did you?'

'I'm not sure,' she murmured. 'Perhaps you should …'

'Try it again?'

She nodded, staring into his dark eyes. 'Uhuh.'

Ben laughed softly, then suddenly she found the world was tilting oddly upwards. No, she was falling backwards. Onto the sofa, safely cradled in his arms.

'Oh,' she managed to gasp.

But that was the last thought she was able to formulate, for the next second his mouth covered hers again and he was kissing her hotly.

Pippa kissed him back, perfectly eager to take things further, and shifted so the hand stroking up and down her spine could do so with even more freedom.

Oh, it was a lush kiss. 'Mmm,' she said against his mouth, exploring his tongue.

Somehow he had found his way under her top, and was stroking one of her nipples through her bra. Then her top and her bra were both on the floor. She moaned, very hot in the face.

'You want this?' Ben muttered, burying his face in the warm cleft between her breasts.

'Oh yes,' she agreed, not bothering to hide how sweaty and flustered she was getting. 'Very much so. Though this doesn't change anything. I still dislike you.'

'Understood.'

His arm hooked around her, holding her steady, then she felt the long glide of her skirt zip being undone. *Oh. My. God.*

'Pippa,' he murmured appreciatively, stroking her bottom. 'I'm so glad I'm not your cousin.'

'It does seem f ... fortunate, doesn't it?'

He turned towards her, one leg pushing relentlessly between hers, and she felt a sudden hard bulge against her thigh. Wow, she thought, her ears starting to steam slightly, that's a pretty impressive package. Pippa wriggled a curious hand down between their bodies and felt the stiff outline of ...

Good grief, was there anywhere he didn't keep a gun?

In her mind she seemed to catch the fleeting strains of Bond music. Was she being seduced by an expert?

She tried to remind herself that her great aunt was in the next room. That dangerous men – possibly with guns – were out there right now, looking for them. That she barely knew this man, and besides which found him very opinionated and disagreeable. But it was no use. The clever sod was just too good at kissing. His kisses were drugs, closing her mind to everything but the mind-altering chemistry happening between them. Her head was spinning. And his hands seemed to know exactly how to touch and stroke, how to find those secret little places ...

'Oh Ben,' she whispered, 'oh no!' Her hands clenched in his hair. 'I mean, yes … Oh yes, please.'

She was woken suddenly some hours later by Ben stirring beside her on the bumpy sofa. She reached out for him, groping appreciatively for his hip, but he slipped away from her naked body. A broken spring *boinged* somewhere in the depths in honour of his departure.

Shocked by the sudden cold, Pippa sat up, reaching for the scratchy blanket. To her dismay it smelt even more strongly of fish. 'Ugh.'

She turned sleepily, to see what he was doing, and was surprised to see him pulling on his jeans, his face grim.

'Ben? What is it?'

He hushed her with a frown, shaking his head, then pointed at the door and made little walking motions with his fingers.

She squinted at him. 'You want to go outside for a walk?'

He shook his head violently, still not speaking, then stuck two fingers together in a gun shape and pretended to shoot her in the head.

'That's not very complimentary,' she said crossly. 'Was the sex that bad?'

Furious, he bent and clapped a hand over her mouth. 'I heard a sound outside,' he hissed in her ear. 'And a car engine. I think they've found us. So shut up!'

Her mouth opened in a silent 'O' and she stared up at him, then nodded quickly.

He turned and reached for his T-shirt, which was hanging off the lamp in a decidedly decadent manner. When he pulled it down over his head, she saw that the heat from the bulb appeared to have scorched a rough dark circle just where his left nipple was. He glanced down at it, annoyed. Though it looked rather hippyish and fetching on him, actually.

Slowly her brain caught up with the stark reality of his

message. The gunmen had found them? They were right outside?

Her heart thundered as she grabbed up her clothes, scattered in various places around the dilapidated sofa, not bothering with her tights and unable to find her knickers, but pulling on the rest as quickly as possible. Where the hell were her knickers?

By the time she was dressed, Ben had his shoes back on as well. He was standing beside the door, listening hard, the gun back in his hand.

Pippa stood by the sofa, tense as a bowstring, unsure what to do. She was cold and still barefoot. She could put her heels back on but if she had to make a run for it, they would only hamper her. There had been a few unfortunate incidents in her past involving high heels and flights of stairs, and adding evil gunmen and darkness into the mix would be asking for trouble.

Should she wake Aunt Evelyn? Was it that serious, or had he just heard a random noise from outside and was being cautious?

Ben unlocked the door very slowly and carefully, then opened the door a crack and looked out into the dark building below.

Pippa watched him, and it hit her in a sudden wave.

She had been to bed with Ben Shakespeare tonight – assuming that was his real name, of course. Well, not bed technically. But it would sound odd to say she had 'been to sofa' with him. Anyway, they had had sex together. Her and him, naked and naughty on the sofa. And no springs, miraculously, had poked into her to ruin their lovemaking.

Lovemaking?

She was not in love with him, she told herself sternly. But he was a massive improvement on Roddy. No contest, in fact. For a start, Roddy had totally lacked stamina, which Ben possessed in, ahem, abundance. Though the gun thing was a drawback, she had to admit. Sex was such an eye-opener; she was not sure she could be entirely happy with a man who went to bed with a gun strapped to his …

Suddenly a shot rang out below, a sharp and unmistakeable *whizz-ping-thud* of metal against metal.

Someone was shooting at them!

Before she had really understood what was happening, Ben thrust his hand through the gap, fired his gun three times in rapid succession, then jerked his hand back inside and slammed the door.

They were under attack.

Frozen with shock, Pippa stood there like a half-dressed shop dummy. With her skirt on backwards and no knickers.

Ben, having locked the door, turned to her, his eyes very dark. He must have been able to see the panic and consternation on her face. 'Sorry, Pippa, could you help me with something?' He was so self-reliant; she could see that it cost him to ask her even that.

Get a grip, she told herself. *He needs you.*

She nodded, stepping away from the safety of the sofa where she had been cowering during the shots. 'What … what can I do?'

'Can you shoot?'

'I told you, I was on the netball team at school.'

'A gun?'

'Oh.' She hesitated, then shook her head. 'Sorry. When I play darts, people stand in front of the board to avoid being hit.'

'Okay.' He threw a lightning glance about the room from under darkly frowning brows. 'Help me shift this table against the door.'

He was already dragging it across the floor. She rushed to help. There were shouts from below. Then the noise of feet on the steps leading up to their hideout. The men would be there any second. Gangsters, with guns. It was like a scene from a movie, only not very entertaining. How many were out there? At least three, by the sound of it. Maybe more.

They slung the heavy table, surface-side first, down against the door like a barrier.

'What else?' She looked about, panting. 'The sofa?'

'Not yet, I'll use it from back here.' He turned the sofa over with one brutal kick, then stood behind the upturned back, aiming his gun at the door. His gaze sought hers without preamble. 'Right, you need to go into the other room now. Look after your aunt. Put the bed against the door, the drawers, anything you can find.'

She didn't want to leave him.

But at the same time she didn't want to get shot.

It was a dilemma.

One of the men hammered on the door, then pushed against it forcefully. There were shouts and swear words, then more hammering.

'But what about you?'

'I'm staying out here.' He checked his watch, his voice tense. 'By my calculations, the team should be here any minute. I rang headquarters again earlier, while you were asleep. They said the team would be coming from Glasgow by helicopter. So there's a good chance … '

The men outside had started shooting at the lock. Pippa put her hands over her ears, the noise was deafening. The door to the bedroom opened and Aunt Evelyn emerged, still fully clothed but with her hair wilder than ever, her eyes bleary with sleep.

'Wh … what on earth's going on?' her great aunt demanded, staring at them both. 'Is it an earthquake?'

'They've found us,' Ben told her.

'Oh good God,' Aunty Evie said faintly, then looked at Pippa, her eyes narrowing in disapproval. 'Dearest, your skirt appears to be on backwards.' She bent to retrieve something from the floor. 'And are these your … knickers?'

Holy hell.

'Erm, thanks.' Pippa snatched the offending article

away from her – a wispy white thing with lace, thank goodness, not the embarrassing big red Christmas pants she had hesitated over that morning – and hid it behind her back. 'I was using them to … erm … They fell off when …' She met her aunt's stare. 'My mind's a blank.'

The kicking and hammering started again, and the door began to bulge in a distinctly sinister manner. Like it was about to give birth.

Ben turned to face their attackers. 'Quick, turn the light out.'

'You want the light out?' Pippa repeated. Her brows shot up. 'Ben, this is hardly the right time for – '

'Turn the light out, then get back inside the bedroom,' he interrupted her crisply. 'Both of you. Barricade yourselves in. And don't open that door for anyone but me.'

It seemed he was determined to be a hero.

Inside the bedroom, Pippa turned the crumpled bed upside down and pushed it against the door, as instructed, then added the small pine chest of drawers as an afterthought. It was not much of a barricade. Actually, it was more like trying to hold back the tide with a bucket and spade. But it was the best they could achieve under the circumstances.

Aunty Evie armed herself with a shoe. 'They'll never take me alive,' she insisted, wild white hair tumbling about her shoulders.

'That's what I'm afraid of,' Pippa muttered.

Suddenly, the hammering stopped outside. A moment later there was an almighty crash – the final assault on the door, she supposed – followed by the grating sound of the large table being pushed across the floor, possibly under the weight of several men.

Ben's gun spoke sharply, several times. That was when Pippa realised why he had wanted the room in darkness. The light from behind the men as the door opened would have given him a momentary advantage, shooting at them before they could pinpoint his location.

A hail of gunfire followed, amid confused shouting.

Pippa stood like a statue, hardly daring to breathe as she listened to the terrible silence that seemed to stretch out forever afterwards.

Had Ben been shot?

Then, overhead, came the sound of an engine. Blades whirring. It grew louder and louder until it was deafening. A helicopter!

There was a series of thumps on the roof right above them, and a voice shouting something on a loudspeaker that she could not quite make out. More rapid gunfire, but this time further away, perhaps even outside the building.

Aunty Evie lowered her shoe, her eyes gleaming with triumph. 'It's the cavalry! We can open the door now.'

Pippa was less convinced. 'Not yet,' she reminded her. 'Ben said not to open the door until he told us it was safe.'

They waited in anguished impatience for another ten minutes, listening to the muffled noise of shouts and engines from outside. Would he never come back, Pippa wondered?

What if … What if he was dead?

She bit one of her nails nervously, and was rewarded by a sharp tap on the shoulder by Aunt Evelyn.

'No biting your nails, dear. Such a bad habit.'

At last, there was a quiet knock at the door, then Ben's voice said, in rather weary tones, 'Pippa? Evelyn? You can come out now. It's safe. My back-up's arrived and the men are in custody.'

She shoved aside their makeshift barricade and dragged open the door, throwing herself into Ben's arms. 'Oh Ben!' She had not realised until that moment just how strong her feelings were for him. 'You're alive! You're alive!'

The lamp was on again, illuminating the room. She

could see a trail of blood near the door, and one of the table legs had snapped in two. Papers and debris lay across the floor.

Not that much of a 'safe house' really, she thought. Not that it was Ben's fault the gangsters had found them. Some criminals would stop at nothing to avoid jail time, even murdering innocent old ladies to safeguard their identities.

Ben winced as she hugged him, then gently pushed her away, holding her at arms' length. His brows were arched sardonically, and she felt a little hurt. Had their night together meant nothing to him but a way of whiling away the time?

'Was I not supposed to be alive?'

'Well, you were outnumbered,' she pointed out, a little crossly. 'And outgunned.'

'And I hadn't had much sleep,' he conceded, with a mocking smile that had her colour up again. Damn him. 'Yes, fair enough.'

A noise made her turn, startled, her nerves still on high alert. Two broad-shouldered men in ski masks and dark clothing, both carrying guns, came through the doorway. But she guessed from the casual way Ben nodded at them that they were police officers and known to him.

'All finished here, Ben?' one of them asked, glancing round at the chaos of the room before holstering his weapon.

'Yes, just about.'

'Well done, laddy!' her great aunt was saying. She clapped him on the back a few times with her shoe. 'You did a grand job tonight. A grand job, I say.'

He winced again, but put his arm about her shoulder. 'Thanks, Evelyn. I don't think anyone else will bother to come after you. Not after this. But we'll double your protection anyway. Until the trial date in January.' He took her shoe away as she continued to hit him with it playfully, and handed it to Pippa. 'Perhaps you might like that back on your foot now? I'm sure Pippa will oblige.'

As he turned away, he staggered slightly, and had to lean on the back of the sofa to keep himself upright.

'Ben?' Pippa followed him, horrified. 'Are you hurt?'

He smiled tightly, indicating his left shoulder. 'It's nothing, really. Just a flesh wound. I'll get it looked at once I've got you two safe home.'

One of the men shook his head. 'We'll take it from here, Ben. The ambulance crew are waiting for you below.'

'It's not necessary,' Ben began, but the other man interrupted him, clearly his superior officer.

'Ben, you know the rules. Get yourself some medical attention. I'll see these ladies have a safe escort home.'

'Yes, sir,' Ben said formally, then shot Pippa a quick look, his expression unreadable. 'Goodbye then.' He smiled at Evelyn. 'It's been a pleasure, Evelyn.'

'So I believe,' her great aunt said tartly, glancing at Pippa, but smiled anyway. 'Thank you for everything, Ben. I wouldn't have missed it for the world. Such an adventure. And at Christmas too. You were my best elf ever!'

Ben said drily, 'Yes, the past few weeks in your shop will stay with me for life. Oddest Christmas I ever spent.'

And with that he was gone. Forever, Pippa thought mournfully. And he'd been her best ever too.

The next day, with the last triumphant sale of Christmas Eve still ringing in their ears, she and Aunt Evelyn sat down to Christmas lunch together. It had been an exhausting week, followed by a nerve-wracking night – though Pippa still had fond memories of some of it! – and although both of them really just wanted to sleep, today was what it was all about: celebrating Christmas as a family. So gifts had been exchanged in the late morning after a marvellous lie-in listening to the church bells ringing in the town, then they had listened dutifully to the

Queen's speech on television while the dinner ticked over in the oven. Now it was time to eat, drink and be merry. (Or prepare themselves for the obligatory post-turkey indigestion, Pippa thought, eyeing the delicious spread with misgiving.)

'Pink champagne, Aunty Evie?" she asked, tilting the bottle over her great aunt's champagne flute. 'Say when.'

Evelyn sat with her lips pursed shut until the champagne was almost over-flowing, then gave a satisfied nod. 'That'll do for starters.'

Pippa slid the heavy champagne bottle back into the ice bucket, sat down and stared at the table between them, laden with food and decorated with a gorgeous festive centre piece of holly and red berries, with an elegant red-hooded Santa in the middle. The turkey itself was huge and golden from the oven, just basted in glistening juices, and surrounded by vast numbers of crisp roast potatoes. There were deep bowls of Brussels sprouts and carrots and roast parsnips, plus a gorgeous cranberry and nut stuffing, and of course oodles of thick gravy.

'There's so much food,' she groaned, helping herself to another tasty parsnip. 'It looks and smells amazing, Aunty Evie, but to be honest we can't possibly eat all this. We'll burst!'

Aunt Evelyn, looking tired but pleased with herself after another rocketing festive season in the shop, carved a thick slice of turkey breast for herself, then poured gravy over her meal. 'I know, an almost obscene amount of food, isn't it?' She chuckled, seemingly undisturbed by the task before them. 'But don't worry, we can always offer some to those two nice boys outside.'

The two undercover policemen on duty outside the house looked rather forbidding, Pippa thought, but seemed cheerful despite the guns they were secretly carrying. 'Just in case,' the officer in charge of Aunt Evelyn's case had said. And it was a relief to know they were not alone now that Ben had gone, even if there was something odd about Christmas lunch under police supervision.

Pippa ate a Brussels sprout ruminatively. She had never liked that particular vegetable, but Christmas was not Christmas without Brussels sprouts. 'I hope Ben's alright. He said a flesh wound, but … it could have got infected.'

'Och, you don't need to worry about that man. He's a very capable sort. Ex-SAS, you know.'

She blinked, shocked. 'No, I didn't know. Seriously?'

'Oh yes,' her great aunt went on, smiling as she tackled a large roast potato. 'That man probably eats flesh wounds for breakfast.'

'Sounds a little indigestible.'

'And wrestles alligators for a hobby.'

Pippa put down her knife and fork and eyed her great aunt suspiciously. 'Now you're just being silly.'

'Am I, dear? Well, you probably know him better than me.'

Pippa flushed. 'I … What makes you … ? No, don't answer that.'

'I won't, then. Pass the cranberry sauce, please.' Aunt Evelyn took the little silver pot, shaped like Santa's sleigh, and doled out a large dollop of thick red sauce bursting with fresh cranberries. 'But one thing I will say is *this*. You never know what's going to happen next with some men.'

'Meaning?'

But Aunt Evelyn would only smile mischievously and shake her head.

A moment later, a knock at the front door made Pippa start, almost knocking her glass of pink champagne over. Gosh, her nerves were still not quite steady.

'That'll be one of those policemen, I expect,' she said, picking up a side dish of chestnut stuffing on her way to the door. 'I'll give them this to pick at in the car. They already turned down my offer of coming in for lunch. Having a sit-down Christmas lunch would inhibit their field of fire, apparently.'

But it was not the police at the door. Or rather, it was, but not the two officers on duty outside.

'Ben!' she exclaimed, and tried to hug him with the glass food bowl forgotten between them. To her horror, she felt tears well up in her eyes. It was silly, she had only known him about a week, and only slept with him once – though it had been pretty memorable! – and now she was in danger of going all gooey over him. 'You … you've come back. I mean, come in. Please. It's marvellous to see you again. I was so worried.'

'You needn't have been. I told you it was nothing.' He showed her his arm in a sling under his festive – and abs-hugging – green woollen sweater. 'They patched me up at the hospital, then I had to go for debriefing. But when I rang the shop yesterday to check how you were, your aunt invited me for Christmas lunch. So here I am.'

'That cunning old bird! She never said a word to me.'

'But you're pleased to see me?'

She bit her lip, not wanting to give too much away but feeling all warm and quivery under that very direct gaze. 'Maybe a little.'

Ben stepped into the narrow hallway and shut the door firmly, blocking the interested gazes of the two undercover policeman sitting in their car outside. He looked down at the glass bowl she had been crushing to his chest. Some of the food was clinging to his sweater.

'Something for me?' he asked softly.

'Stuffing.'

'I enjoy stuffing,' Ben said, picking a few moist crumbs off his sweatshirt. His gaze did not waver from hers as he licked his fingers. 'Very tasty.'

'Come and sit down, there's plenty more where that came from. We did a cranberry and nut one too.'

'Sounds delicious.' His dark gaze locked with hers. 'Pippa, after lunch, I thought we might try … a game.'

'Oh.'

'You've gone pink. What kind of game do you think

I'm suggesting?' he asked mockingly, head tilted to one side as he studied her flushed cheeks.

Her heart was hammering, and she could not take her eyes off him. Really, he was insanely gorgeous, especially wounded. 'I don't know. Scr … Scrabble, maybe?"

'Wrong guess,' he said lightly, handing over a parcel wrapped in bright Christmas paper with a big red bow. 'Perhaps this will give you a clue.'

'For me?' She took the parcel in pleased surprise, then her eyes widened as she saw what was on the wrapping paper. Were those lady elves … naked? And cavorting with Santa? 'Erm, I don't think you should show *this* to Aunt Evelyn.'

'She's the one who recommended it, actually,' he said calmly.

She unwrapped the parcel while he waited, then gasped again at what she found inside. Her face must be scarlet, she thought, trying to still her wildly beating heart. 'Oh gosh … it's … *huge.*'

'It'll fit.'

'How can you be sure?'

He smiled and kissed her lingeringly on the mouth, until her head was spinning and her knees were weak. 'Because I did,' he whispered.

Aunt Evelyn appeared at the doorway to the dining room in time to save her from replying, a Santa hat crowning her wild white locks and brandishing a Brussels sprout on her fork.

'Och, Ben, so there you are at last. Merry Christmas to you, laddy!' she exclaimed, a huge grin on her face at seeing them together. 'Thank you so much for saving our lives. A more handsome – or welcome – lunch guest I could not imagine.'

'Merry Christmas, Evelyn,' he said, kissing her on the cheek. Then he smiled at Pippa, looking sideways at her confusion from under his long lashes. 'I think I forgot to wish you a Merry Christmas, Pippa.'

'M … Merry Christmas!' she managed to reply, hurriedly wrapping up her gift before her great aunt could see what it was.

But Aunt Evelyn's loud tutting told her the old lady already had a good idea what was going on. 'Come on, you two lovebirds, enough billing and cooing. Plenty of time to enjoy your presents while I'm sleeping my lunch off. Right now the turkey's getting cold, and no one's pulled my cracker yet. Who wants the wishbone?'

Ben slipped his arm about Pippa's waist as they followed her into the dining room. 'Just wait till you see me in my sexy Santa outfit,' he murmured in her ear. 'I have handcuffs too. After the Christmas pud, okay?'

'Saucy!' Pippa whispered, and giggled.

She set a place for Ben beside her at the dining table, and he pulled up a chair, smiling at her.

'A toast!' Aunt Evelyn raised her glass of champagne, waiting until Pippa had filled a glass with pink bubbly for Ben as well. 'To the possibility of a threesome,' she announced boldly, and winked.

THE ODDEST LITTLE
CHRISTMAS CAKE SHOP

CHAPTER ONE

Rosie Redpath would probably have walked straight past the mouth of the arcade except for the fact that she could smell gingerbread.

She loved the smell of gingerbread. So warm and spicy and festive. It made her think of winter nights and chestnuts roasting by the fire and sleigh bells and all things Christmassy.

But it was not Christmas, of course. Not for a good few weeks.

A lone snowflake drifted past on its way to a melting death on the pavement. Rosie hung about to watch it perish, then turned into the arcade and made her way past the other shops towards Minchin's Cake Shop.

It was cold today. But cold enough for snow? In November?

She shrugged deeper into her thick yellow hoodie, aware that she was procrastinating. She had a decision to make, and decision-making was not her strongpoint. She liked to have a range of choices, naturally. But as soon as one decision is made, most of the alternative choices would be lost forever. And some might never come her way again. So she preferred to avoid hard decisions whenever possible.

Once upon a time she had known exactly what she

wanted, and thought she knew how to get there. Work hard to get good qualifications at school, work even harder for a good degree, land a good job in the world of work. But those days were gone, and she felt lost in this post-university world bristling with unexpected options and depressing dead ends. Should she stay in London with her nan or leave in search of a new life, as her parents had already done? Should she get a job or go travelling again? Should she eat a doughnut with jam, or a sugary one with a hole in the middle?

She simply did not have the answers.

Rosie gazed down at the glorious window display of cakes in Minchin's Cake Shop. For perhaps the first time in her life, she had absolutely no idea what she wanted, though taste-testing some of the options might prove interesting.

But was *this* the right place for her?

Stepping into the dusty, echoing, black-and-white chequered hall of the Cherry Court Arcade had been like entering another world. Not a promising sign, she had thought. Thanks to the ongoing recession, most of the shops were closed now, rusted metal shutters drawn down permanently or handwritten signs in the window that warned of erratic opening hours. Those that were open today had a sad and neglected air, paint peeling from dirty wooden door frames, the window displays unloved and lacklustre, price tags faded over time, the shop interiors behind them gloomy and half-empty.

The only establishments open for business today included a train enthusiasts' haven, a dimly-lit barber shop, and a haberdashery run by a middle-aged woman of stern demeanour who peered out through a porthole rubbed in her dirty window as Rosie passed in ripped jeans and trainers, her bright yellow hoodie an affront to the drab air of the place.

And then there was this cake shop.

Roughly halfway along the enclosed arcade stood

Minchin's Cake Shop. Just in case passers-by were in doubt, its front door had been propped open and a large chalkboard set out on the pavement beyond the arcade to lure passing trade out of the failing daylight. Prettily-drawn cupcakes and cream horns – at least, she hoped they were cream horns – danced about the artful scrollwork on the chalkboard.

OPEN 10AM – 4PM: MINCHIN'S CAKE SHOP.

Rosie had stopped outside the cake shop, ostensibly to admire the window display but also to make what might be the biggest decision of her life so far. And she was still standing there, staring in amazement.

A rich and glorious smell of baking drifted out through the open door, enlivening an otherwise dull and chilly afternoon. Not a dreary, everyday, bread-baking smell, but an enticing smell reminiscent of childhood, of cakes and muffins and misshapen biscuits, of licking the bowl as a kid, of aprons and chocolate vermicelli and edible balls.

There was a cornucopia of baked goods on display in the window. Cakes and scones and biscuits had been laid out neatly on old-fashioned, wooden trays tilted towards the glass, with spaces only where some lucky customer had managed to take the last of a particular item. Beyond them, on white plinths designed to show off their stately and elaborate icing, rose cakes of an altogether grander order, multi-tiered wedding cakes and birthday cakes and, of course, Christmas cakes.

Christmas cakes were a promise of something fabulous to come, she always thought. Rich and nutty and deliciously fruity, a reminder of fertility in a bleak, winter landscape. A token for the mouth that rebirth is just around the corner. The curls and tufts of their elaborate icing always reminded her of snowy scenes on Christmas cards, of frozen lakes and skating rinks, of snow and everything turned white for wintertide.

Perhaps it was just as well such fruitcakes were only eaten once a year, she thought. One generous slice of

Christmas cake was probably enough for most people. When the cake had been made by an expert, that was. Someone who knew how to produce a rich taste of Christmas in every fragrant mouthful without it being too much, without overloading your senses.

Below the festive cakes were the everyday cakes, and what a superb selection, Rosie thought, momentarily dazzled as she scanned what was on offer.

There were cream puffs and horns and slices, sprinkled generously with sugar and filled with oozing white cream. Lemon drizzle cake in ordered slices, gorgeously sweet and sticky-looking. Croissants, both plain and almond, soft and inviting. An array of plain, cheese, cherry and fruit scones on assorted platters, sloping and brown-topped. Doughnuts rings next to jam and vanilla custard doughnuts, all of them golden-brown and rolled lavishly in sugar. Wickedly delicious individual treacle tarts beside vast, family-sized apple pies crusted with beads of brown sugar, outrageously fat and chocolatey eclairs, plus fairy cakes of various descriptions, perfect crumbly macaroons – her personal teatime favourite – iced fingers and buns with and without raisins, then flapjacks, Danish pastries, *pains au chocolat*, blueberry muffins, triple chocolate muffins, lemon muffins, carrot cake slices with buttercream frosting ...

She looked up in a dream of sticky creaminess, dazed by the choices laid before her, and read the bold, handwritten sign in the window.

HELP WANTED. ENQUIRE WITHIN.

Yes, this was the place. She would have preferred to interview for a job with a major bakery chain or catering company, or even a restaurant. But Minchin's Cake Shop, humble though it seemed in this dusty arcade, had one serious advantage over the other jobs she had ringed on the print-out from the Job Centre.

It was close to home.

'Now, Rosie, don't you worry about me,' her nan had

insisted stoutly when she first announced she would be looking for a job close to their small, high-rise flat. 'I can look after myself. Been looking after myself for the past thirty years with no problems. Goodness, a talented girl like you, straight out of university … You should be making a packet in some posh city job. Laying on sushi for the Prime Minister and his cabinet. Not wasting your life round here with an old lady like me.'

Rosie could not deny the sense in that. She needed a well-paid job. Her university loan would not pay itself off, and besides, she had been out of university since May and was bored and restless. A major restaurant or catering company would suit her perfectly; she was keen to work, and had a good second-class degree in Catering – it might have been a First if she could have given up her busy sideline in theatre, but she had loved working backstage on student productions too much to sacrifice it for a better grade.

However, a big pay packet and career prospects were not her only considerations in looking for a job. Since her crazy parents had relocated to Australia last year, her poor nan had been left to fend for herself, an old lady living all alone on the twelfth floor of a high-rise block. She might still be mobile and have all her faculties, but Nana Nora was eighty-six years old, knocking on for eighty-seven soon, and not always in robust health.

Rosie thought her nan needed someone around the house, however much she might protest that she wanted to live independently. Not only to help out with housework and groceries, which a home help outfit could provide if their budget would stretch to it, but for that most basic human need of all: *company*.

And an old people's home was out of the question. They both knew that.

'I'm not ready for that nonsense, my girl. Not by a long shot. Besides, everyone knows these old folks' home are full of doddery old gents and birds without a full set of marbles, and I'm still perfectly *compos mentis*,' her nan had declared, glaring at Rosie in a dangerous fashion when she suggested the move. 'You'd have to carry me out of here feet-first.'

So she had moved in with Nana Nora in late summer, after coming back from a wonderful but exhausting six week trip to visit her parents in Australia. It was only a two-bedroom flat, a little cramped and still furnished the way it had been back in the seventies, all brown and orange abstract pattern wallpaper, and fluffy rugs with lava lamps, but she had soon fallen in love with the place – and life with Nora.

She had always secretly thought her parents to be fussy and narrow-minded. But Nana Nora was a real hoot, especially as a house-mate.

A thoroughly disreputable octogenarian, Nora wore pink tartan leggings and borrowed Rosie's hoodies, and danced while making her supper, and watched late-night sex programmes on satellite telly, and played practical jokes on Rosie, like hiding all her underwear in the pan cupboard or jumping out on her in the dark.

'It's been a fantastic summer, but I do need to get a job,' she had told Nora in the end. 'A local job. So I can keep an eye on you.'

'Well, you know how I feel about that. But if you must take a local job,' her nan had said reluctantly, 'I saw one advertised recently that might suit a girl of your skills.'

'Hmm?'

'Catering. Well, a bakery.'

'Whereabouts?'

'Maybe bakery is pushing it a bit. It's a cake shop, really. In the shopping arcade behind the canal.'

Rosie had looked up from her breakfast, surprised. 'I didn't even know there was a shopping arcade behind the canal, let alone a cake shop.'

'That's because you don't know everything.'

'Don't I?'

'No,' her nan had said firmly. 'Don't go thinking a university degree means you know more than me. It just means you *owe* more than me.'

'I feel crushed.'

'It's called Minchin's Cake Shop and it's been there forever. Well, it's been there for as long as I can remember. Which is a very long time. Now, don't make that face, cheeky monkey. You'll be my age one day and then you won't find it so funny to creak when you walk.' Nana Nora had drawn an odd squiggle on one corner of the newspaper she was reading, then torn it off and thrown it across to Rosie with a flourish. 'Here. That's a map of where it is. They're asking for help in the window.'

'What do they want help in the window for?'

'Ha, ha.' Nora had downed her nearly-cold tea in one gulp, then shuddered. 'Ugh. I'm setting to work on that new jigsaw puzzle this afternoon. So you've no reason whatsoever to stay here and keep me company. Go out and get some fresh air. And come back with a job.'

'But I studied catering.' Rosie had eyed the upside-down squiggle with misgiving, suddenly unsure. 'It was all accountancy and administration. Business plans, logistics, that kind of thing. Though I think we did one module on baking in the first year,' she finished vaguely.

'Oh, I don't imagine they'll let you loose on the cream cakes, sweetheart,' her nan had said comfortably. 'I expect they need someone for basic clean-up. You'll be washing the windows and sweeping out the bakery and scrubbing down work surfaces, that kind of thing.'

Rosie stared at her aghast. 'Seriously? Three years of a degree course and I end up as a scrubber?'

'It's either that or … what was the other local job you looked at?'

'Hand-made sausages.'

Nora looked at her with raised brows. 'Can't miss that opportunity. Perhaps I should have applied for that job myself. What wouldn't I give to spend all day on a production line squeezing puréed pigs' testicles into the lining of a sheep's stomach?'

So here she was, squiggled map in hand, standing in front of Minchin's Cake Shop. And though she could not quite see herself mopping up and scrubbing down, it could not be denied that the place smelled delicious.

'Can I help you?' a voice asked politely. 'Have you come about a cake? Or are you just browsing?'

Rosie turned, startled, and had to lower her gaze substantially to find the woman's face. 'Oh, hello. Yes, I've … erm … come about the job.'

The woman addressing her was only about four foot nine or ten to her five foot six, and looked a decade or so younger than her grandmother, probably somewhere in her late seventies. She was wearing an immaculate white blouse buttoned up to the neck; it matched her white hair, drawn back into a stern but elegant chignon. An equally spotless white apron was protecting her blouse, and her severe knee-length black skirt. She was wearing dark tights, and on her feet were smart black leather loafers.

The woman had the kind of taut, pinched face and watchful eyes that suggested she had seen too much suffering in her life, and could not forget it, though she deeply wished to.

'The job?'

Rosie pointed to the sign in the window. 'Help wanted.'

The woman looked her up and down for a moment, her small dark eyes bright as buttons, then shook her head. 'Oh no, I'm sorry. No, no, no.'

'No?'

'No,' the woman repeated regretfully, then disappeared back inside the shop with a muttered, 'Thank you for coming. Good afternoon.'

I knew I should have rung first, Rosie thought.

Though perhaps it was the bright yellow hoodie. And the ripped jeans.

She turned away, secretly relieved. She had not wanted the job anyway. She knew next to nothing about baking. And it sounded like too much hard work, all that scrubbing. Not that she was afraid of hard work, but she had envisaged herself in a more managerial position. Spreadsheets, promotional ideas, logistics, that kind of thing. So perhaps she had deliberately dressed down and not rung first.

It was probably for the best. She had two left hands in a kitchen, her nan had once exclaimed, rescuing yet another burnt offering from a smoking oven; she might have ended up poisoning half the neighbourhood.

'Wait.'

She was nearly outside in the chilly November air again when The Voice called after her. It stopped her walking, drew her up just short of the street. It was not the woman's voice again, sharp with disapproval. It was a deep, authoritative male voice that echoed about the dusty arcade, bouncing off tiled floor and walls, seemingly coming from nowhere like the voice of a deity.

'Come back a minute, would you?'

The cat that had been grooming itself on the black-and-white chequered tiles leaped up and darted away at the sound of that voice. The lady in the grimy-looking haberdashery peered out through her igloo porthole again, eyes suddenly wide with curiosity. The grey sky hung there with breathless anticipation. Rosie experienced an odd feeling too, somewhere in the pit of her stomach, a kind of churning sixth sense that warned her to be rude and keep walking.

Yet she did not keep walking. She turned to see who had spoken. Though when she did, Rosie was tempted to bolt like the cat and never come back.

CHAPTER TWO

Oh my goodness, she thought, her eyes widening at the sight of him.

'Sorry?' she said, eyes fixed on the man's face, but trying desperately not to ogle him. More than she already was, anyway.

'Mrs Minchin dismissed you too soon. I want to see your CV.'

Want, not *would like.*

Her nan would have accused him of being rude. Rosie mentally corrected him, then just as silently accused him of being too damn sexy.

'Did you hear what I said?' he demanded.

She stared at him, unable to process his words quickly enough to think of a response, and the man standing in the doorway to the cake shop stared back at her. Like it was a contest to see who would blink first.

She lost hands-down.

Blink. Blink. Flutter, flutter, blink.

'My … CV?'

'You did bring one, I suppose?'

She found herself walking back towards him. Just a few faltering steps, but hell, she had to see this man more closely. He was dressed in a clean bakers' outfit of checked trousers and white tunic buttoned almost up the neck, just one flap left open at his throat. His hands were clean, but there was a smudge of flour on one cheek. Hardly sexy

84

attire, she thought drily, and yet ...

She had never felt so attracted to a man before in her life.

Bareheaded, he was tall and dark, narrow-hipped, something lithe and graceful about the way he held himself. But menacing too, his dark eyes watching her the same way a cat watches a pigeon.

'I didn't think I would need one,' she said. 'Someone mentioned the shop, and I was passing anyway, so I thought ... '

'You came unprepared?'

He was looking her up and down, hoodie-covered head, ripped jeans, trainers, then back again, exactly as the older woman had done. Only with a fixed, intent stare. Mrs Minchin, he had called the woman. She glanced again at the name above the shop. The proprietress. But if she was the owner, how was he able to override her decision to reject a job application?

'Not unprepared. Just unready. Like that medieval king,' she added, unable to help herself, 'Ethelred the Unready.'

Now it was his turn to blink.

'Look, no offence, but I should probably be going,' she said uneasily, uncomfortable under his stare. 'To be honest, I don't think Mrs Minchin really liked the look of me.'

She started backing towards the gloomy afternoon light at the end of the arcade, trying not to think of it as a tunnel.

'And really, who can blame her? She's right, of course. I'd stick out like a sore thumb in that shop. With her, and you, in that ... ' and she waved a hand vaguely at his checked trousers and white tunic, 'astonishingly *clean* Best of British Bake Off get-up,' she finished.

A muscle jerked in his cheek. The one with the smudge of flour on it.

'I'd prefer to be the judge of that,' he told her calmly,

and then crooked a long finger in her direction. 'Come back here, little mouse. Let's sit down inside and talk.'

'Talk?'

She raised her eyebrows at the word. While he was crooking his long finger at her, she had been thinking of something quite different, probably involving melted chocolate and satin sheets and oh, some very naughty badness that she ought to be spanked even for considering.

Then his other word hit her. 'Mouse?' she suddenly repeated, outraged by its inaccuracy. '*Mouse?*' She rolled up the sleeves of her hoodie. 'I don't think so, buster.'

His slow smile was not what she had been expecting. Or wanted, frankly. He was the kind of man she needed to stay away from, the kind she had flirted with in the past and come away bruised and smarting. This man was like a stick of dynamite; he should have DANGER written all over him.

She had needed him to turn away in disgust, had wanted him to be offended by her martial attitude, but it seemed he was not.

Instead he laughed softly, then held out his hand. 'Come inside, I want to show you something.'

Oh good grief.

Incredibly, she found herself walking back towards him, her eyes locked on his. But all the way she was trying to dissuade him. 'I'm not suitable for the position, honestly. I put on weight just looking at a cream cake, like I've *inhaled* it or something. And I can't bake. I'm a menace in the kitchen. I even managed to burn bread rolls on my degree course.'

He raised his eyebrows. 'You have a degree, then?'

'Catering.'

She was in the doorway, then inside the shop. There did not seem to be any other customers. She had probably scared them away with her too-bright hoodie. The space was narrow and the smell of cakes and icing so delicious, she felt almost light-headed. Like an airborne sugar rush. The diminutive Mrs Minchin had vanished, she noticed. Down some convenient rabbit hole perhaps. In her place was a cheerful lad in spectacles and apron, wearing plastic gloves for serving.

'Hello,' the young man said, smiling at her broadly. He looked about her age, or maybe a little younger. 'I'm Colin. Have you come about the job?'

'No,' she said firmly.

He stared. 'Oh, I thought … '

'We can talk in the back,' the man insisted, ignoring him, and led her through a narrow doorway before she could say anything else.

She followed him down three steps into another room; it was large and airy, white-washed walls, clean and modern, and lined with immaculately clean stainless steel trolleys that gleamed under strip lighting. It was nothing like the old-fashioned exterior of the shop, and wonderfully warm after the chill November air outside. Perhaps even a little uncomfortably hot.

This was the bakery itself, she realised, inhaling seventy-five thousand calories as she passed a stainless steel trolley of cakes, including about a hundred freshly-piped eclairs gleaming with still-damp chocolate strips.

'You can't possibly sell all these cakes through that little shop,' she commented, and almost bumped into him when he stopped suddenly.

'Of course not. We do outside catering as well. It's a very lucrative business. Brings in far more revenue per annum than the shop ever could.' He turned, looking into her face. 'Though you're right, of course. With a degree in Catering, you're wildly over-qualified for the position being advertised.'

'Which is?'

'Sweeping up back here, cleaning the shop, maybe serving customers too during our busy times.'

'Oh, I'll take any job I can.'

'I thought you didn't want to work here?'

She felt heat in her face. 'I just thought … '

His eyes narrowed on her face. 'Did Mrs Minchin offend you out there? Is that your issue?'

'I don't have an issue. I don't do issues.'

'Then what?'

She drew a sharp breath. 'I'm sorry, I don't even know your name.'

'Pyotr.' He held out his hand again and this time she took it. They shook hands, his strong thumb resting on top of hers in a firm grip. 'Pyotr Wood.'

'That's an odd name.'

'Not really. It's a foreign version of Peter.'

'Foreign?'

'My father was British. Hence the Wood part. And I was born here in London. But my mother was Russian. She preferred the Russian Pyotr to the British Peter. So I got landed with it.'

He finally released her hand, and Rosie pulled it back, nursing her hand against her chest like his handshake had wounded her.

'A Russian mother. Fascinating.'

She felt like collapsing in a heap right there on the floor of his bakery and drooling insanely. The air was throbbing with his sex appeal. Or perhaps it was the heat and hum of his industrial-size ovens affecting her. Somehow she managed to keep smiling in a polite and definitely non-certifiable way.

'And yours?' he prompted her.

'Oh no, my mother was – is – from Basingstoke.'

He looked at her. 'I meant, your name.'

'Oh, right.' She thrust her hand back out at him. 'Rosie,' she said with a flourish. 'Rosie Redpath, that's my name.'

He lowered a cool gaze to her outstretched hand. 'We've already shaken hands.'

'Of course we have.' She turned on her heel,

thoroughly embarrassed and pretending to admire his bakery. Though it was actually rather gorgeous. Like him. State-of-the-art. Nothing like the humble shop front in the arcade. 'So, you work for Mrs Minchin? Or perhaps you're her partner?'

She looked back when he did not answer. His eyebrows were still raised, two strong dark arcs above eyes that watched her with faint hauteur.

Rosie stammered, 'Not … romantic partner, of course,' and looked hurriedly away again. 'I meant, her *business* partner.'

There was a long and awkward silence.

Oh God.

'Not that there's anything wrong with a May-September romance,' she pushed on, floundering horribly through the social quagmire into which she had inadvertently blundered. 'Personally, I think love between the generations must be very rewarding. Not that I have any solid experience of that myself. But my nan is knocking on for ninety, and even she gets a bit flushed when Richard Armitage comes on the telly in his, you know, those tight-fitting pantaloons or whatever it is they wear in costume dramas that show the outline of … Anyway, I think most women Mrs Minchin's age would love to … ' She hesitated, fumbling for the right words in the silence. 'Would be thrilled, in fact, if a man like you … wanted to … with her … *Especially* a man like you.' She grimaced, not daring to look at him. 'You know what, I'm just going to shut up now.'

'Excellent idea,' he said drily, then held out a straight-backed plastic chair. 'Very pleased to meet you, Rosie. Now sit.'

Now sit.

Like she was a dog.

With considerable self-control, Rosie restrained herself from woofing or panting or letting her tongue loll out, and sat down on the chair like any normal person would in a job interview situation. Pyotr pulled up another plastic chair and sat down opposite her, leaning forward slightly as though there were a table between them instead of space. She played with the zip on her hoodie, avoiding his watchful gaze.

'How old are you?' he asked at last.

'Twenty-three. How about you?'

He looked taken aback, then said, 'Twenty-eight.'

'Capricorn?'

'Scorpio.'

'I thought so.'

Ignoring that, he continued smoothly, 'And how long since you left university?'

'Too long.' Rosie told him about her parents emigrating, and her trip to Australia, and her nan's uncertain health, and then saw his eyes begin to glaze over and finished hurriedly, 'So I'm looking for a local job if at all possible.'

Pyotr asked about her degree course, the modules she had taken, her other qualifications, then asked if she could provide references and certificates to back it all up.

'Of course,' she replied promptly.

He talked to her for a while about their present commitments in terms of outside catering, and his plans for gradual expansion.

'Though you only want me for sweeping up?' she asked, unable to resist teasing.

'Every job here is important,' he said seriously.

'You sound very thorough.'

'I like to keep an eye on everyone.'

She looked at him, fascinated despite herself. 'You never told me your position here. It's Minchin's Cake Shop. Not Pyotr's Pastries.'

He smiled slowly.

'So,' she pressed him, 'are you the boss?'

'Mrs Minchin is the owner. We formed a partnership last year though to expand the business, so I suppose, yes,

I am the boss. Jointly with Mrs Minchin.'

Several people came into the bakery, wearing white uniforms, and he rose at once to speak to them. The newcomers were two young men, one with gingerish curly hair, the other blonde and rosy-cheeked as a cherub, neither of them any older than she was, and a slender-hipped woman of about thirty with chestnut hair cut very short and a large, generous mouth that curved rather too warmly into a smile when Pyotr greeted her.

A girlfriend as well as a colleague?

Rosie stood too, feeling distinctly shy and a little self-conscious. Did she want to work here? They seemed a lovely bunch of people. But there was something about Pyotr; she could not put her finger on it, but it unnerved her. Not just his animal magnetism, which was drawing her in with every word he spoke, but something beyond that, a strange, glorious, alluring darkness that spoke to the light inside her. She had always preferred the light to the darkness, sunrise to sunset, martini to navy rum, yellow to red. But sometimes she felt a curious absence right at the heart of her. Perhaps a little darkness was exactly what she needed, and just turning the light off every night was no longer enough to fill that gap …

'Sorry about that.' Pyotr came back and put away the chairs. He folded his arms across his broad chest, looking at her. 'So? You want to work here?'

'Can I let you know tomorrow?'

Pyotr raised his eyebrows, clearly taken aback by that response. 'No,' was presumably not a word he heard very often.

'Sorry,' she said frankly, 'but I do need to have a think about it. Besides, I feel like we've been talking for hours, and I'm sure this must be taking up your valuable time.'

'You don't like what you see?'

She felt heat in her cheeks and did not know where to look. Good grief. Yes, a thousand times yes, she liked what she saw. And she would not mind touching what she saw too.

'It's … not that,' she said awkwardly. 'Honestly, I love the shop, and the bakery, and your plans for the future sound fascinating. But … '

He shook his head, arms still folded. 'I won't let you walk out of here without making a decision.'

Rosie felt trapped at once. A decision? Just like that?

She turned on her heel, looking around at the bakery. Like the little shop beyond the narrow doorway, this was a beautiful place, and the scent of sugar and spices and baking in the air worked on her like a drug. But something was nagging at her, warning her to say no, or at least take a little longer to consider the offer.

She thought of her ambitions at university, her wish to work for a major company after her degree, somewhere with plenty of opportunities for training and advancement. It was her dream to run her own catering business eventually, or possibly run a top restaurant somewhere in central London. If she took a small-time job like this, she might as well give up that ambition. Yet if the cake shop had a thriving sideline in outside catering, there would be opportunities for her to learn some useful new skills for the future.

Best of all, she would be able to stay close to her nan. And that was why she had come here today.

But could she keep her hands off this man?

'Okay, it's a yes,' she said at last, since he seemed disinclined to let her escape without a decision. 'I would like to take the job.'

He nodded, straightening. 'Be here at five tomorrow morning,' he told her coolly. 'I'll sort out a uniform for you. What are you, a size ten? Make sure your hair's up. This is a food environment. Thanks very much for applying. And welcome.'

He held out his hand, and she shook it in a daze. Same warm palm, strong thumb, the firm grip. Oh goodness.

'Five?'

'I'll be here at four. This is a bakery,' he reminded her drily. 'We start early.'

'When do you sleep?'

'Sleep is much over-rated,' he said. 'I can think of much better things to do at night.'

She stared.

He hesitated. 'That came out wrong.'

A shrill child's voice echoed along the tow-path outside. She watched, surprised, as Pyotr turned his head at once to listen, his expression suddenly intent, his large hands clenched into fists at his side. Then he seemed to make an effort to relax, fists slowly unbunching.

Smiling in a forced way, he guided her out of the bakery. 'Well, see you tomorrow.'

Rosie said goodbye and made her way through the shop, then out into the arcade hall, Pyotr a few steps behind as though seeing her off the premises. Like he thought she might nick a cream horn on the way out …

The afternoon felt chilly after the balmy, unnatural warmth of the bakery. There were still a few flakes of snow about. She hugged herself deeper into her hoodie.

'Wait,' she said as Pyotr turned back into the cake shop, then forced herself to meet his dark gaze when he looked round, his expression a little haughty. 'What made you … ? I mean, sorry, but Mrs Minchin gave me a resounding no. She obviously didn't like what she saw. I was nearly on the street when you called me back.' She paused. 'I'm just wondering why you did that.'

He hesitated, then said, 'You reminded me of someone, that's all.'

'Who?'

'It doesn't matter. Someone I knew a long time ago.'

'And that's why you asked me back?'

'That,' he agreed calmly, his expression unreadable, 'and something else.'

She stared. 'What else?'

But Pyotr simply said, 'Five o'clock sharp tomorrow

morning.' Then he disappeared back inside the cake shop, leaving her curious and frustrated, staring at the space where he had been.

CHAPTER THREE

Pyotr watched her leave, then turned to Sarah Minchin who had emerged from the back office. 'What did you think of that applicant?'

'I thought my opinion was unimportant.'

He waited.

Sarah shrugged, sensing perhaps that he would not be drawn into an argument. Not this afternoon. 'She's very young. What kind of experience can she possibly have?'

'She's older than Colin.' The boy blushed at this reference, and busied himself rearranging the already perfectly arranged cakes in the window display. Pyotr frowned at Sarah, feeling a burst of impatience at her narrow-minded approach. 'Besides, what kind of experience does a person need for sweeping floors?'

Sarah looked at him. 'Don't pretend she won't be helping out with food preparation inside of five minutes,' she said tartly. 'I've seen that look on your face before.'

He digested that in silence, then asked softly, 'What exactly is that supposed to mean?'

Looking a little nervous now, Sarah shrugged. 'Nothing. Look, we agreed that you would handle hiring and firing, so let's just leave it at that, shall we?'

Pyotr glanced at the boy again, who took the hint and discreetly slipped into the bakery. 'I want to know what you meant by that,' he pressed her.

'Only that the last two girls didn't last very long.'

He should not be surprised by this full-frontal attack. Sarah Minchin had been icy and distant for some weeks now, showing her dissatisfaction with their business arrangement. He said nothing in response though but stood, staring at her. For the first time since he had bought into her ailing bakery, he wondered if it was time to move on.

Sarah raised delicate eyebrows at his silence, then glanced over his shoulder as the old-fashioned shop door bell jangled.

'There's a customer coming in,' she said in a low, warning tone, then added when he did not move, 'I've left some invoices on your desk. Perhaps you could deal with them before you leave?'

He glanced round at the customer, a smiling young mother with a buggy, housing an infant rendered all but invisible by snug, white woollen layers, and heard himself say, 'Of course.' He nodded to the young woman, who was dark and attractive, if a little over-made-up. 'Good afternoon, madam.'

The customer looked back at him admiringly. 'Hello,' she replied shyly, and with a flash of irritation he caught Sarah Minchin's knowing expression.

Damn her.

Back in the sanctuary of his bakery, Pyotr sent Colin scurrying back to serve the young woman with the buggy. He knew Sarah Minchin would not bother, rarely seen out front these days, serving customers. Though she did like to busy herself with the window and cabinet displays, and with suggestions for what other goods and services they could sell. Some days he thought she was a little too busy, given that it was his expertise and investment that had kept her old family business from closure.

But he could not blame Sarah for wanting to protect her own. It was certainly what he would do, in her place. Business was one thing. Family and heritage, those were things that should always be preserved and honoured.

Safely alone, Pyotr strode to the window that overlooked the canal. This view was one of the reasons he had chosen to invest in this shop.

Across the oily, greyish waters of the canal stood the local children's home. It was a large, red-brick Victorian building in shabby condition, a ten-foot wire fence set around the small compound like something from the Cold War. Through its tiny black striations he could see children at play in the yard and hear their excited, high-pitched shouts. School must have recently kicked out, he thought, watching them. Some were quite young, only primary school age, but now and then he caught a glimpse of a brooding teenage face staring out through the fence, or a couple of hunched figures leaning against the wall together, arms folded.

He stood there another few minutes, listening to the shouts of the children, then turned away and began to untie his apron. He had been awake since three o'clock that morning, as usual, and had even snatched forty-five minutes at the gym late morning. After dealing with the paperwork, and making any necessary payments to suppliers, he would go home for the day.

It did not take long to go through the stack of invoices. Nonetheless, he felt distracted. His thoughts kept returning to Rosie.

He had glanced at the woman outside the shop when he first heard her and Sarah speaking, then stopped and looked again. Wavy gold-blonde hair tumbling gracefully past her shoulders, large and expressive blue eyes that flashed fearlessly before Sarah Minchin's tyranny, and a smile that could melt the polar cap.

And that face …

'Marina,' he muttered again, this time to himself.

His first impulse had been to run down the arcade after her, to catch her in his arms, to kiss her until neither of them could stand. But of course the woman had turned at his shout, staring and astonished, and he had seen at once that she was not Marina. That her eyes, while also blue, were warmer, less vulnerable and defensive. Nor was she as slender and petite as Marina. He had sensed a strong, athletic figure under the casual hoodie and ripped jeans, and suspected she could handle herself in a tough situation without turning to a man for help.

No, she was no fragile porcelain doll, this woman, despite her fairy-tale beauty. The way Rosie held herself suggested muscular training and determination, and when he had spoken to her at length, face-to-face, his impression had been one of bloody-mindedness masquerading as ambition.

She was, in fact, the very antithesis of Marina, while looking startlingly like her.

Had he finally lost his senses? He had offered the woman a job, for God's sake. A job far below her qualifications, references unseen. And for what? So he could see her face every day and indulge in this helpless desire for something impossible, something long-vanished, like the fool he was.

Perhaps he thought the sight of her every day would work in his wound like a speck of grit in the delicate flesh of an oyster, slowly growing a pearl. Instead it was more likely to drive him mad.

Pyotr closed his eyes for a moment, head bowed. Let the old desperation fill him for a moment. Then he shook it off and straightened, reaching for his wallet and keys.

It was dark by the time Pyotr left the shop, and his journey home – a short walk to the tube, then forty minutes by train – was accompanied by whirling flakes of snow. His flat was cold and silent when he let himself in. It was a secured residence block, but out of habit he checked all the rooms to be sure there were no intruders. Then he stood in the kitchen-diner, looking through his mail.

Mostly bills and junk mail-shots. But one envelope caught his eye. He tossed the others aside onto the marbled white work surface, then took a knife from the cutlery drawer, using it to slit the envelope open.

It was another brief report from the firm of private investigators he had hired on arriving back in London last year.

Pyotr scanned the contents of the report, which were dry and to-the-point, then carried the letter through into his bedroom. Hidden under one of the polished oak cabinets beside his generous kingsize bed was a box file. He took this out. opened it on the bed, and filed the letter inside for safekeeping. He took a moment to glance through the other contents of the file before closing it again, though he knew them all by heart. Then he replaced the box, carefully moving the cabinet back into position to conceal its hiding-place.

Such precautions were probably unnecessary, he thought, standing there in the darkness of his bedroom. But he did not like to take chances. Not where his past was concerned.

Stripping off, Pyotr strode naked to the bathroom and stood under a hot shower for ten minutes. It was a long shower by his standards. He tried to make it perfunctory but could not help himself. The powerful jet of water cascading down his back bore away his weariness, but it seemed the mundane act of soaping himself had taken on new and disturbing erotic overtones since his encounter with Ms Redpath.

It was hard not to recall her face without imagining her in the shower with him, bold and naked, running a soapy hand over his pecs. Rosie Redpath. She sounded like a cartoon character. A cartoon character with the figure of a pocket Venus. He thought of the sparkle in her blue eyes, the generous curve of her mouth, and turned slowly under the hot water jet, bowing his head, starting to breathe heavily.

Could Rosie be as innocent as she looked? He sincerely hoped not. He could just imagine the two of them together. Her smiling eyes inviting him on.

Since hers were not there, his own hands had to do the dirty work for her, soaping his torso first, and then drifting ever lower …

'Do you want me to rub that in for you?'

Startled, Pyotr turned to find Rosie standing right behind him in the bakery. Jerked out of his daydream, he hoped he was not blushing, though he could hear his own heart hammering away guiltily.

She looked even more delectable today in her spotless white uniform, dustpan in one hand, brush in the other. Her hair was peeking out from under her mop cap, one wayward fair strand curling like a question-mark over her smooth forehead. Like a young Victorian maid servant, eager to please the master of the house.

Which was sexist and politically incorrect, he told himself sternly. Yet found himself unable to shake the image.

'I know all the techniques,' she continued, innocently oblivious to the lascivious turn of his thoughts. 'How to rub in, how to knead, and how to make it rise. And not just because of that bakery module I took. My nan's an amazing cook. She taught me everything she knows.'

'I don't doubt it,' he said drily, but shook his head. 'I'm sorry, but no. It's only your first day on the job, Miss Redpath, and I've already told you, no hands-on work until I'm satisfied.'

'Satisfied?' she echoed.

He hesitated. 'That you've completed your training. Besides,' he added, pointing behind her, 'you've missed a bit.'

She turned, staring, and her face fell when she saw a tiny cluster of pastry fragments still on the bakery floor beneath one of the units. 'I'm so sorry.'

'Never mind, just get on with it.'

'Of course.' She hurried over with her broom. 'But do call me Rosie. And if you ever need any help rubbing in …'

'No need,' he told her brusquely. 'We tend not to hand-make anything these days, except very special bespoke items. It's mostly done by machine.'

'Machine?' She glanced over her shoulder, biting her lip in chagrin, that blonde curl bobbing as she swept hard with the little brush, bending over with the dustpan. He tried in vain not to return to his sordid daydream. 'What a shame.'

'Isn't it?'

'Though using a machine must get the job done a lot quicker than if you only used your *hands*.'

He agreed with a strangled, wordless noise.

'Even the kneading?' she asked

'Especially that.'

'What about the Christmas cakes?'

'They've all been made in advance.'

'Of course.'

'Though we'll be starting on the icing next week. That's still done by hand here.'

She looked round at him, her cheeks flushed. 'May I help with that, then?'

He could not help smiling at her enthusiasm. It was rather sexy. Sarah Minchin had disapproved of the speedy departure of the past two helpers he had hired, but although he knew she feared he was a seducer, the girls had actually left because he was too hard a task-master for them. They had not shown even a flash of Rosie's enthusiasm for the job, and had merely wanted to do as little as possible.

'I don't see why not. If you can demonstrate enough

skill during your training, you might even be let loose on a few cakes all by yourself.'

'Thank you,' she told him, her eyes glowing. He could not help being captivated by their warm, excited expression. 'I do love Christmas cake. The gorgeous heady smell of them, the taste on your tongue, the firm, rich texture …'

'Remember though,' he warned her, 'the Christmas cakes we make here may turn out very differently to any you've made at home.'

'I remember covering mass production machines on my course. But I never saw myself actually working anywhere that used them.'

He looked at her, his brows raised. 'You regret taking this job?'

'Goodness, no,' she said at once, her face horrified, and turned to face him, stopping her sweeping. 'I just mean, I originally intended to … That is … '

He smiled when she faltered, perfectly well aware what she had been thinking. 'You saw yourself taking a very different sort of job after university.'

Rosie nodded.

'Life can be like that,' Pyotr remarked lightly, though his heart was beating hard. He was remembering another girl in another city, half a life away, how he had told her all his secret fears and regrets, laid himself bare for her. And she had broken his heart. 'In my experience, things rarely go according to plan. But it seems to me that nothing happens without a purpose.'

'You really believe that?'

'I do,' he agreed softly. 'In fact, I'd stake my life on it.'

CHAPTER FOUR

Monday morning, Rosie was looking at the wall clock in silent anticipation of an early lunch break when Colin burst into the bakery, grinning broadly. 'Look out of the window!' he told them.

His expression absorbed, dark head bent, Pyotr said nothing but continued to monitor the kneading machine.

Rosie, who had been cautiously constructing a vast Yule Log ready for layering with chocolate cream, frowned round at the young man. 'What is it? Is Santa delivering early?'

'Just look out the window,' Colin insisted, 'and you'll see. It'll be worth your while, I promise.'

Still wearing her plastic gloves for hygiene, Rosie wandered across to the window that overlooked the canal. There was nobody out there. The wintry canal path was deserted, except for one abandoned supermarket trolley and a few birds pecking in a disconsolate fashion at the frosty ground. The world looked dark and gloomy, although it was only late morning.

'Okay,' she said slowly, 'what am I looking at?'

Colin came to join her, pointing into the frozen sky. 'See that?'

She watched as a single white flake drifted erratically past the window, followed a few seconds later by another, then another, then another in ever-increasing quick succession.

'It's starting to snow,' she said blankly. 'So what?'

Colin stared. 'So what?' he echoed, then shook his head. 'Haven't you seen the weather forecast?'

She had been so tired after her first week at the bakery that she had spent most of the weekend half-asleep, mostly under a duvet on the sofa watching the telly while her nan plied her with warming soups and toasted sandwiches.

'Sorry, no.'

'It's going to snow all this week. Heavily. *Really* heavily. They say some London transport networks may be shut-down if the snow gets really bad.'

She thought of her nan sitting at home in their cold flat, and hoped she had put the electric fire on. Snow was always rather lovely at this time of year, with Christmas just around the corner, and all the shop windows full of brilliant light displays, but it was also undeniably cold.

Besides, Rosie did not like the idea of having to wade through tons of the white stuff just to reach work every morning.

'It's a good thing I live locally, then,' she replied, but sighed, watching as the falling flakes thickened and began to whirl excitedly above the dark waters of the canal.

Pyotr cleared his throat right behind them, and they turned hurriedly to find his forbidding gaze on their faces.

Rosie felt her eyes widen, alarmed to find herself in such close proximity to the boss. Not for the first time, she noticed how good Pyotr smelled. Better than one of her nan's home-made meat pies, she could not help thinking hungrily.

Though it was not a comparison that entirely worked, she realised, quickly adjusting her thinking. If her boss was a meat pie, he would not be a stout, homely pie like her nan would make, the kind that does best drowned in rich gravy and served with chips. No, Pyotr would be a cordon bleu venison pie with perfectly sculpted shortcrust pastry and a fragrant but tart cranberry jelly encasing the meat. To be served cold on a generous platter, perhaps sliced into quarters and accompanied by a crisp green salad and mustard.

Her mouth began to water …

'Snow,' Pyotr agreed, peering past them through the window. 'Very nice. Meanwhile, there is plenty of work to be done here.'

She gesticulated with a plastic-gloved hand. 'Quite right. Sorry.'

He turned his stern gaze on Colin. 'Is there anyone in the shop? Mrs Minchin? Or have you left the place unattended?'

Colin made some incoherent sound in his throat, then slunk past him on his way back to the shop.

'I thought so,' Pyotr said drily, then looked back at Rosie.

'I was just … ' Her plastic gloves clawed vaguely at the air again. 'Yule.'

'Of course.'

He was still staring at her though. Had she put too much make-up on? Was her mascara running? That would be typical. She was not used to putting on make-up, had gone without it since her teen years when she would have felt naked without her 'war paint' as Nan called it.

Yet since coming to work with Pyotr she had felt an almost compulsive need to look attractive, so out had come all her old eyeshadows and lipsticks, much to her nan's amusement. But her make-up technique was a bit rusty. Besides, she kept forgetting it was there and rubbing her face. That must be why he was staring at her. She probably looked like a panda bear with one black-smudged eye.

'What's the matter?' she could not help asking.

He flicked one of her ears. 'Dangly earrings,' he said

softly. 'Completely forbidden in a food preparation area. As I'm sure you know.'

Her face grew hot. She had forgotten all about her earrings. Little silver dangly threads, she had put them on this morning along with her make-up, thinking they made her eyes look brighter.

But then he had asked her to help with the Yule Log.

'I'm so sorry,' she said promptly. 'I'll take them off when I go for my lunch break.'

'Very well.'

Pyotr stood aside to let her return to her work station too, but then alarmed her even further by following. What was up with him today?

She hoped he was not planning to sack her. She had started to enjoy this job, limited though it was career-wise. And Nan loved all the free or reduced buns and cakes she kept bringing home after work. Though perhaps that was not such a good thing for either of them. They could end up looking like a couple of hippos if she did not take steps to curb their full butter scone habit.

He stood to one side, watching her work as she smoothed on the rich chocolate cream using long, deft strokes across the cake. It was unnerving. She kept hoping he would go away, but the annoying man did not budge, watching her in silence.

'How are you settling in?' he asked her at last.

'Good, really good.' Great, she thought. Her voice was now high and squeaky. Like she was a cartoon mouse. A cartoon mouse trapped in a lab cage for experimentation by a mad scientist. A very *sexy* mad scientist, she corrected herself wildly, and tried not to imagine Pyotr in a white coat with an electric probe in his hand. 'I mean, last week was great too. Getting to sweep the floors and wipe down surfaces. But I'm so glad you've decided to trust me with … '

'Food?'

'Yes, exactly,' she agreed, beginning to roll up the Yule

Log with small, neat turns and not too tightly, as she had been taught by her nan. 'There's more job satisfaction in a Yule Log.'

'Gently does it,' he said softy, coming close behind her.

She hesitated, which was fatal.

'Here, let me show you how.' He put his hands over hers to demonstrate. His hands were gloved too. The two layers of see-through plastic rubbed together uneasily, a smear of chocolate cream crushed between them. He manipulated her fingers, helping her to finish rolling up the Yule Log. 'Like this. And this.'

God, he was so leaning in so close, she could feel his whole body pressed against hers.

Harassment in the workplace!

Except this was very far from harassment. More like helpless encouragement. Rosie was leaning back against him too, eager to feel …

'Goodness!'

He dropped his hands at her exclamation and stepped back. 'What is it?'

She turned, staring down at his black apron, but it discreetly concealed everything below the waist. 'I thought I felt … something … very big … and … '

'Hard?' he supplied.

She nodded, swallowing.

Pyotr fished a gloved hand under his apron, fiddled there for a few seconds, and then whipped out a large black phone handset.

'I put the shop phone in my pocket earlier. Forgot it was there.' He glanced at the screen, which was lit-up, then lifted the handset to his ear, frowning. 'Hello? Mrs who? Yes, sorry about that. Erm … wrong number.'

'Pyotr?'

He turned, and Rosie saw his face harden at the sight of Mrs Minchin in the doorway to the shop. 'Yes?' he said shortly.

'Could I have a quick word?'

He put down the phone and nodded to Rosie. 'Carry on as I showed you,' he said, then left the bakery.

Rosie turned back to her delicious-smelling, extra-rich chocolate Yule Log, head bent, a little trembly. This attraction to her boss was getting out of hand. Or *in hand*, actually.

She remembered how his fingers had pressed against hers, so warm and confident, and imagined them pressing other places too, rather more privately, maybe on a soft, cushion-strewn bed in a darkened room. But of course he would never do that. Despite the way he had leaned against her body, she could still see that coolness and distance in his eyes too, the standoffish demeanour she had noticed on their first meeting.

Pyotr was a man who kept other people at arms' length. Especially women, she suspected.

She had dated a few boys in school, though it had never been serious. Her first proper boyfriend had been at university. Simon. Fair-haired and skinny, a first year on her degree course, he had been a whizz at chess but not much good at sex. Probably an inexperienced virgin like herself, she thought, with the benefit of hindsight. Not that she had really known what to expect in the bedroom. Indeed, it was not until bearded mathematician Allan had introduced her to advanced sexual technique in her second year – anything beyond the straight missionary position was "advanced" to her at that stage – that she realised what Simon had not been doing.

That had been an eye-opener.

Then she had met Karl in her third and final year. Attractive, smooth and so plausible, he had soon persuaded her into bed. Their brief fling had only lasted a few heady and exhausting weeks. But they had covered most of the positions in Karl's much-thumbed paperback edition of the *Kama Sutra* by the time she snuck round to his flat one afternoon and discovered him in bed with his next-door-neighbour, a chemist called Paul.

Another eye-opener.

With both eyes now sewn firmly wide-open, and propped up with matchsticks for good measure, Rosie had sworn off men after Karl. Her final examinations had been beckoning by then, anyway.

But Pyotr was not another hapless, philandering student. And she doubted that he was a bisexual predator, though of course you could never tell.

Still, he was the boss.

And that was always a no-no.

Okay, she had only just entered the post-university world of work. But Rosie had been reading *She* and *Cosmo* since she had been old enough to reach them down from the Women's Magazines shelf in her local newsagent, and over the years she had devoured dozens of dubious articles on ethics in today's workplace, most entitled something enticing and salacious like, "Banging The Boss" or, 'What You Need To Know About Sex To Avoid The Sack".

She finished rolling the vast Yule Log, then cut the roll carefully into similarly-sized sections, exactly as Pyotr had shown her a few days before. They would be decorated individually and sold as mini-logs.

Colin wandered in. 'Going for lunch?'

Sometimes they went to the pub a few blocks down for lunch, and sometimes they just ate shop sandwiches outside the back door to save money.

'Yes, I've just finished here.' She covered the Yule Log sections, then wiped her hands. 'Is it still snowing out there?'

'Coming down harder now, yes.'

She smiled at him, pulling off her cap. 'Pub or sandwiches?'

'Pub, in this weather. I'm not risking frostbite sitting out there.' Then Colin frowned, staring at her. 'Hold on, weren't you wearing two earrings this morning?'

She felt both ears, expecting to feel two dangly earrings there. Her left ear was bare. 'Bloody hell.' She looked down, peering around the floor of the bakery. 'It must have fallen out while I was working. Here, help me look, would you?'

With a resigned expression, he dropped to his knees and started looking under the trolleys and work surfaces. 'When did you last have it?'

'I'm not sure.'

Then she remembered Pyotr flicking her dangly earring. Her left ear, she was sure. The one without an earring now.

It could not have fallen into the Yule Log she had been rolling, could it?

Rosie turned and stared suspiciously at the covered tray of Yule Log sections, and tried to imagine what would happen if someone bit into a dangly earring while enjoying a delicious chocolate treat from Mrs Minchin's Cake Shop. She suspected dental work might be required, at the very least. Perhaps a trip to casualty at the worst.

Was there a jewel in the Yule?

She panicked. How long would it take to check each log for inadvertent jewellery? And would she have to open each one and ruin them all in order to find it?

Her stomach pitched. 'Oh crap.'

'What?'

It was unlikely that Colin could be trusted with her guilty secret, so she fibbed instead. 'N … nothing. I just remembered something. A birthday.'

Colin grinned, looking up at her. 'A birthday? You have a brain like a butterfly, did anyone ever tell you that?'

'No,' she said, offended. 'And I don't.'

Determined to find the errant earring on the floor rather than in one of the individual Yule Logs, Rosie joined him on her hands and knees by her work station. The bakery floor was not surprisingly cool but at least it was clean, thanks to Pyotr's obsessive mopping routines.

'The bloody thing must be around here somewhere,' she muttered, patting the linoleum floor with her plastic gloves in ever-increasing circles.

He peered under a metal trolley. His eyes narrowed and he pointed. 'Aha. What's that?'

'What?'

'Something small and sparkly.'

She knelt next to him and bent as low as she could. Her fringe flopped into her eyes. She still could not see what he was pointing at. 'Sorry, where are you looking?'

'There, there!'

'Seriously, I can't see … '

'Brain like a butterfly, blind as a bat.' Colin sighed, then shuffled beside her and leant right down, pointing right along her eye-line. 'That. Shiny. Thing. There.'

She squinted. 'Oh, that. That's a … a silver ball-bearing, I think. Aniseed flavour. We were sprinkling them on the sticky cones earlier. With hundreds and thousands. That one must have rolled away.'

At that moment, someone cleared his throat behind them. It was not a happy sound. 'Forgive me, am I interrupting a special moment?'

Colin lurched to his feet with a muttered expletive, leaving Rosie flushed and embarrassed, down on her hands and knees, staring over her shoulder at their boss.

Pyotr was not looking amused.

'I have nothing against members of staff becoming close,' he remarked tersely, 'but I expect any romantic interludes to take place outside work hours, and certainly never on the bakery premises themselves. You must have broken half a dozen hygiene regulations already.' He was looking at her in a particularly forbidding manner. 'You're lucky I don't sack both of you on the spot.'

Rosie's face could not have been any redder if she had been leaning on a hotplate. Bloody hell. Pyotr thought they had been enjoying a spot of nooky on the bakery floor. And his disdain for her tarty behaviour was undisguised.

'It's not what it looks like,' she faltered, scrambling to her feet and brushing down her knees.

'Really?' His eyebrows arched.

Colin murmured something about lunch and slipped hurriedly away, leaving her standing there alone. My hero, she thought resentfully.

'So,' Pyotr said more softly, his hard gaze snagged on hers, 'if you two were not getting down and dirty on the bakery floor, what precisely were you doing?'

She put a hand to her ear, then stopped herself just in time. Earring, she thought. Chocolate cream. Yule Log. Casualty.

He would probably sack her for having lost her earring while preparing food too. And this time, she would actually have deserved it.

'It was ... Colin and I ... ' She stared, then blurted out, 'I thought I saw a ball-bearing.'

'A ball-bearing?'

'Under that work station.' She pointed. 'At the back.'

Pyotr looked at her, a muscle jerking in his jaw. Then he stepped past her, effortlessly rolled the metal work station away from the wall, and looked down behind it. There was a three-second-silence, then he said, 'Broom.'

Rosie fetched the broom and handed it to him.

He used it to hook out the ball-bearing, which rolled innocuously between their feet, then pushed the work station back into place. They both stood gazing down at the small silver ball-bearing.

'Aniseed, I think,' she commented. 'Tricky little things.'

'Hmm,' was all he said, but she saw his thoughtful gaze return to her face, and knew he was thinking much the same about her.

CHAPTER FIVE

Unfortunately, Rosie did not get a chance to unpick the Yule Logs in search of her lost earring, as Mrs Minchin came in shortly afterwards and chased her out, snapping, 'Time for your lunch break, Miss Redpath. And you can take an extra half an hour today. Mr Wood and I have things to discuss.'

She glanced wistfully across at the covered tray of Yule Logs, then shrugged and nipped into the ladies' on her way out to fetch her coat and bag.

The toilet doubled up as a cloakroom and changing area, being essentially two rooms divided by a metal wall, the cloakroom part having a handy row of hooks on the wall as well as a sink and hand-dryer, and a low wooden slatted bench for sitting on or storing outdoor shoes. She nipped into the loo as well, and almost locked herself in again.

'Damn thing,' Rosie muttered, wrestling with the stiff lock on the loo door. But it gave in the end, as it always did, and she escaped the cloakroom just in time to hear raised voices in the bakery.

Were Mrs Minchin and Pyotr arguing again?

She hoped the business was not in trouble. Because she was beginning to enjoy this job.

The shop was busy, as it often was at lunchtime, a short queue of customers waiting impatiently to pay for their rolls and cakes, and to order takeaway hot drinks. Which made it all the more surprising that Mrs Minchin had chosen that time to have a row with Pyotr.

A pale young woman called Paula was serving in the shop on her own, looking flushed and harassed. She glanced at her with wide eyes when Rosie tried to hurry through with her head down.

'Can you help?' Paula asked desperately. 'I'm being run off my feet here. Colin's on his break and Mrs M.'s disappeared somewhere.'

Rosie stopped, dragging on her bright orange woollen mittens. (They had seemed like such a fun choice when she bought them, but from the odd looks she kept getting on her way to work, they might have been an unwise purchase.) She was keen not to waste her precious lunch break, but equally unwilling to leave Paula coping with the lunchtime rush alone.

But it seemed the supreme sacrifice was not to be demanded of her. To her relief Mrs Minchin appeared behind her and all but shoved her to one side.

So rude!

'Get along with you, girl,' Mrs Minchin said sharply, and bustled behind the counter to help serve. Her eyes widened at the number of customers waiting. 'Right, who's next?'

Rosie dashed out of the shop before she too could be pressed into service, and took the back way out of the arcade for once. It led out onto the canal path where snow was falling thickly now, weaving through grey air and paving the ground with a soft, crunchy, white blanket. She loved messing about in the snow, always had since her childhood, and even now found it hard to resist the urge to scrunch up a handful of fresh-laid snow into a threatening snowball. But her woollen mittens would not be quite so warm and comfy when wet, and besides, there was no one to bombard with a snowball anyway.

Then she spotted Colin, leaning against the back wall of the bakery, scoffing down a round pie. One of their own steak and kidney pies, by the look of the red tin foil wrapper.

'Hey, you,' she said loudly, and was gratified when he looked round at her, startled. 'Thanks so much for your support earlier. Nice of you to run away as soon as the boss appeared.'

Colin made a face, trying to speak with a mouthful of pie. 'Th ... thorry,' he managed to say, 'didn't ... mean ... leave you ... lurch. But he ... thcares the ... thit ... out of me.'

'The thit?'

'Thit, thit,' Colin repeated, slightly flushed, spitting out flaky bits of pie. 'Thit!'

She ducked back a step. 'Please, no more,' she insisted, holding up a large orange mitten. 'I don't fancy being showered with steak and kidney.'

'Thorry.'

'It's fine.' She looked hungrily at his bulging lunch bag. 'What else have you got in there? Anything I can have? I didn't dare stop to buy something for lunch. The Minchin came out of nowhere just as I was leaving and I had to dash out before she could force me to serve in the shop. The place was heaving.' She saw his aggrieved look, and put on her most innocent smile. 'I'll pay you back.'

Reluctantly, Colin rummaged in his lunch bag, then brought out a ham salad sandwich. Half of it. 'How about that?'

'Thanks.' She took it, then looked at him. 'Where's the other half?'

'I ate it.'

Nice.

She took a bit. It wasn't bad. 'Thanks, I suppose it serves me right for not bringing something with me from home.'

'We could get chips, if you like.'

Rosie shook her head. 'Not really my thing.'

'Well, whatever you like. Pizza? Kebab?' Colin was

looking at her hopefully. 'You and me.'

'Oh.' She swallowed. 'You mean … A date.'

He shrugged.

'That's really nice of you, Colin. But I don't think I should date anyone I'm working with.'

'Why?'

Rosie stared at him through the falling snow, momentarily lost for words. That had not been the mature response she had been hoping for. How to let him down gently without offending him? Normally she would have been a lot blunter at this point, maybe even mentioned the fact that he still had a touch of boyish acne. But she had to work with the guy, and besides, it was rather sweet to be asked out on a date. She could not remember the last time that had happened.

Suddenly, something wet and icy hit her in the side of the face.

'Ouf!'

She turned, and saw several kids ducking out of sight behind some trees on the other side of the canal towpath. 'Hey, that wasn't very fair. Shouldn't you lot be in school?'

She stooped and immediately scrunched up several handfuls of crumbly snow in her mittens, melding them into one respectable snowball. Not very mature of her, perhaps, but getting into a snowball scrap was better than having to deal with Colin's embarrassing question, especially as she knew he would not like her answer.

'Come on out then, give me a chance.'

Giggling, the kids leaped out and started collecting more snow. They were five of them; they looked about fourteen or fifteen, wearing school uniform. On their lunch break, maybe?

'Take that.' She launched her snowball across the canal, hitting one of them in the back. A girl, who shrieked and darted away behind the trees again.

'Watch out they don't cross the bridge and get you from behind,' Colin warned her, pointing out how close they were to the old iron footbridge.

'Huh, I'll be ready for them.'

He eyed her second snowball with raised brows. 'You really take this kind of thing seriously, don't you?'

'No point going into things half-hearted,' she said, then dodged sideways under a rain of snowballs.

Splat, patter, splat went the enemy snowballs against the wall of the bakery, each one missing her entirely. One hit Colin in the leg though and he shrieked like a little kid. But she emerged unscathed from that round, lobbing her second snowball over-arm as she ran, and watching in satisfaction as it caught one of her unprepared opponents in the back of the head.

'They're gunning for you now,' Colin commented, scraping snow from his knee.

He was right. All the kids were bending to the ground, arming themselves for another onslaught. It looked like some of them had two snowballs apiece. Hurriedly she gathered another few good handfuls of thick snow, crushing them mercilessly into one very large snowball.

'Hey,' a voice said behind her.

She whirled and threw her snowball hard. Right into Pyotr's face.

Rosie gasped.

She clasped her wet woollen mittens against hot cheeks and stared in dismay at the snow dripping from her boss's face.

'Oh, I'm so sorry. So so so sorry. I thought you were someone else.'

With a stony expression, his gaze locked on hers, Pyotr lifted one hand to wipe the remnants of her snowball from his face. A little late though. Some of it had already dripped onto the lapels of his clean baker's uniform. She wanted to laugh but did not dare. Not in the face of his inevitable wrath.

'Evidently,' he remarked.

'Colin and I were having a snowball fight with … ' She

turned, hoping Colin would back her up, only to discover that he had vanished. He seemed to have a knack for escaping awkward situations, she noted resentfully.

'With?' he prompted her.

'With some of those school kids on the towpath.'

He turned in the direction of her pointing hand, his brows twitching together into a frown. 'What kids?'

Dismayed, she realised the towpath was empty.

Pyotr was looking at her oddly. 'Look,' he said, drying his wet chin with the back of his hand, 'if you'd rather work somewhere else, you could just hand in your notice. Not snowball me in the face.'

'Honestly, that was a mistake,' she insisted, feeling wretched. 'I'm so sorry. And I do like working in the bakery. Here, please let me help.' Impulsively, she lent forward and patted his nose a few times with her mitten. 'Better?'

When she lowered the mitten, Rosie noted that his expression had not changed. Which was not a good sign, she decided.

'Since that repulsive woolly object appears to be sodden and covered in ice, no.'

'Oops.'

She wondered where Colin had gone. He was probably watching them from round the corner, wondering if she was being given the sack. It was astonishing to her that Pyotr had not done so, actually. After hitting one of her bosses squarely in the face with a snowball, she ought to be hopping around in a large brown sack by now. But she saw no anger in Pyotr's face, only fading surprise and some other emotion she could not quite decipher. Respect? No, that could not be right.

'I only came outside to offer you this.' He produced a white paper bag, neatly closed with a tuck, and held it out to her. 'Since you did not seem to take any lunch out with you.'

She stared, confused. 'How … thoughtful. You noticed

that?'

Pyotr shrugged.

Taking the bag, she peered inside and found a tuna mayonnaise wholemeal sandwich. It looked freshly-made and smelt gorgeous.

He looked at her. 'You like tuna mayo, don't you?'

'Yes, I love it. But how did you know?'

'Apart from the fact that you've made yourself a tuna mayo sandwich most lunch times since you started working for us?'

She smiled. 'Am I that predictable?'

'You're very far from predictable,' Pyotr said, and a fragment of snow he had somehow missed dripped silently from his forehead onto his shoe.

'You mean the snowball,' she said.

'That,' he agreed, 'and other things. Though I certainly wasn't expecting to be gunned down when I came out to give you that sandwich.'

'I'm really sorry.'

'Forget it.' He looked past her, frowning. 'Is that Colin? Hiding round the corner?'

'Probably.'

A little irritated, Rosie strode round to the corner of the bakery and looked behind the building, fully expecting to see Colin cowering there. She did not like providing a show for her colleagues. But the space was empty. If he had been hiding there, he was long gone now.

'Nobody there,' she said, surprised, and turned back.

Something wet and hard and icy-white hit her full in the face. Rosie shrieked and staggered back, wiping the snow away, then peered past her mittens to see Pyotr grinning at her, his hand still raised.

'I'm afraid you must forgive the subterfuge,' Pyotr admitted. 'But I couldn't think of any other way of defeating you.'

'You rotter.'

'That's one hit apiece,' he said softly, 'if we're keeping

score.'

Pyotr was still smiling when he returned to the bakery.

He could not deny it, he was smitten with the new employee. But then, it would be hard not to find Rosie Redpath attractive. There was her generous smile, for starters, and her quick wit, and her infectious laughter. Then there was her body, perfect for cuddling but sexy with it, invitingly curvaceous. And the fresh, fragrant smell of her hair …

Whenever he was within a few feet of the woman, an overwhelming desire to touch her came over him. He was used to exercising iron self-control over his sexual urges. So it was rather alarming how impossible he found it to keep his hands to himself when she was around. That unfortunate incident with the Yule Log this morning, for instance. The bulge she had felt pressing against her delectable bottom had not merely been down to the phone in his pocket. Though she was not to know that.

Though of course he should not keep giving into the temptation to spend more time with her than the job merited; he was not ready for another relationship, nowhere near ready, and he doubted she would be interested in a one-night-stand. She was too young to see sex as an end in itself, rather than a means to further intimacy. There was such an alluring innocence in her face, he would not have been surprised to discover she was a virgin. In which case it could only end badly if he tried to seduce her.

Just because he had not had any luck with his mission recently, he could not allow himself to forget that he had come back to London and invested in this business for one purpose only. And it was not so he could play baker.

Still, Rosie Redpath did have a charmingly mischievous smile.

His mobile rang and he fished it out of his pocket. Number withheld, the screen said. He hesitated a few seconds, then hit the green answer button.

'Yes?' he asked cautiously.

'It's me.'

He stiffened at the familiar voice, glancing through the door into the busy cake shop. He could see Mrs Minchin bending over the glass counter, and Paula bagging up a cream horn for an old gentleman.

'I'm at work,' he said quietly into the phone.

'I know you are. This couldn't wait.'

'One minute.'

Frowning, Pyotr walked through to his small office. He kicked the door shut for added privacy, then sat down at his desk. The swivel chair creaked in protest as he swung in it. He really ought to fix it.

'Very well, I'm listening. What do you want?'

'We've had a positive sighting. '

'When?'

'Eight-thirty approximately, yesterday evening.'

He sat up, struggling with anger as well as a sudden pulse of adrenalin. 'Yesterday? You should have rung me immediately.'

'I didn't want it to be a false lead. Not after what happened last time. So I decided to go and check it out myself, first thing this morning.'

'And what did you find?'

'Let me read you the details. Have you got a pen and paper?'

'Hang on a second.' Pyotr tore a sheet out of his notepad, then reached for a pen in his top drawer. He did not dare allow himself to feel excitement. Not this time. They had been at this stage before only to find the lead was mistaken or the trail had gone cold. 'Right, go ahead.'

'First, Mr Wood, I need to remind you to go about this cautiously. Not like before. You'll only frighten the horses if you go charging in again without proper preparation. It could put us back months.'

'Understood,' he said impatiently. 'Now give me the

details.'

CHAPTER SIX

'Rosie, are you sure about this?'

'Absolutely,' she whispered.

'One hundred percent sure? Because once we start, there's no going back.'

'I can handle it.'

'Rosie … '

'I can handle it,' she said again, more firmly.

A pair of concerned blue eyes met hers. 'All right, pass me the knife.'

Rosie hesitated, then handed over the knife, which seemed to glint evilly under the lights.

'And the bowl of icing.'

She peered into the bowl of sweet and sticky royal icing they had just mixed into a smooth enough paste for covering a cake. Egg whites and sugar, whipped together with a little lemon juice into a creamy mix, just the right consistency for spreading on top of the Christmas cake. All in the vast, cracked, brown-rimmed, old china mixing bowl her nan always used for such special cakes.

'Thanks for doing this,' she said, hooking a little icing out with her finger and tasting it. 'Mm, gorgeous.'

Her nan grunted, then peered at her from under lowered brows. 'Well, I don't mind helping out. But you ought to be able to remember how to do this without a refresher from me. You've iced a few cakes with me before now.'

'But that was a long time ago, Nan,' she explained, 'and a Christmas cake is special. I want to get this right.'

'Don't they offer any training at this place?'

'Yes, of course. But I want to look good. Really good.'

'All right, all right. Don't squeeze that bowl any harder, it'll crack. That was my mother's mixing bowl.'

Rosie eyed the grim ceramic bowl in her arms with astonishment. 'Seriously? No wonder it's so old and cracked. Should we be using it at all? It probably belongs in a museum. Must be at least a hundred years old.'

'I beg your pardon?'

'Oops, sorry.' She handed over the bowl. 'I just meant … Never mind.'

Her nan made a growling noise under her breath. 'A hundred years old, my backside.'

'Sorry.'

'Eighty, maybe.'

She grinned. 'That twenty makes all the difference, does it?'

'You wait until you're my age, miss. Then you'll be sorry stairs were invented.' Her nan grimaced, rubbing her knee absentmindedly. 'People wear out just like cars, you know. Bits fall off or stop working.' She glowered at Rosie. 'And evenings are when old ladies like me get to relax on the sofa with a pitcher of martini and watch mindless garbage on the television. Not stand about icing Christmas cakes with cheeky, ageist granddaughters.'

'Honestly, I'll make you a pitcher of martini myself when we're done. And I'm sorry your knee hurts. Perhaps if you were to sit down? But this is important. You have shown me how to ice cakes before, but I've forgotten exactly how to do it and … I want it to look as though I already know what I'm doing.'

Nan pursed her lips. 'I don't need to sit down. I'm not in my dotage yet. But I do think I understand what this is all about.'

'You do?'

'What's his name?'

Rosie tried not to blush, but it was like asking warm dough not to rise. There was still time to save herself from further shame though. She opened her eyes very wide, gazing back with an expression of bewildered innocence. 'Name? What on earth do you mean? What makes you think … ?'

'I'm your gran, sweetheart. I'm supposed to know things like this.' She pinched Rosie's chin. 'And if this sudden enthusiasm for icing Christmas cakes isn't over some tasty piece of manflesh, I'm the Queen of Sheba.'

'Pleased to meet Your Majesty,' she muttered, but it was no use.

'Come on. I want a name, at least.'

Rosie struggled a moment, then gave up. This was her nan, after all. What harm could it do? 'Pyotr.'

'Sounds odd.'

'It's the Russian name for Peter.'

Her nan looked astonished. 'Is he Russian, then?'

'Part-Russian, I think.'

'Which part?'

Rosie looked at her stubbornly. 'The good part.'

Her nan shook her head. 'I hope you know what you're doing. He's not one of these Russian gangsters, is he?'

'Gangsters?'

'I watch television, you know.'

'Now you're being ridiculous.' Feeling a little cross, Rosie turned back to the cake on the kitchen table. Though she did not entirely understand why she was cross. It should not matter to her what Nan said about Pyotr Wood; it was not like she was involved with the man, after all. And when that thought brought more heat into her cheeks, she felt even more aggrieved. 'Let's do this, shall we?'

Her nan hesitated. 'Rosie? You're not getting annoyed,

are you?' She rubbed her arm reassuringly. 'I was only messing with you, love. I'm sure he's a very nice man.'

'He's my boss, nothing more.'

'Of course.'

'Cake.'

'Absolutely. Now, let me see …'

Her nan put on a frowning expression, bending to examine the fruit-and-nut-packed Christmas cake. It had been mixed and baked six weeks ago, then kept in a battered old cake tin at the back of the cupboard to 'mature' as her nan had put it. They had brought out the cake with great ceremony five days ago, spread a light and zesty apricot jam across the rich fruitcake, then carefully covered the cake with a layer of marzipan. It had then been replaced in the cupboard, only this time covered with a clean dishcloth to keep it from drying out.

The whole thing now smelt utterly gorgeous and Christmassy.

'Come on then, let's see you ice this cake.'

'But I thought you could make a start …' Rosie protested.

Her nan shook her head, and her white curls bounced cheerily. 'Not if you're going to impress this boss of yours.' She scooped some icing out of the bowl with the broad-bladed knife, then handed it back to Rosie. 'You might prefer to use a spatula, but I've always used a knife for royal icing. Want to give it a try?'

Rosie took the knife, wishing her nan had the large, soft plastic spatulas they used at work. But this would do. She made a few tentative passes across the cake, leaving the marzipan covering smeared with white, then returned to the mixing bowl for more icing.

'Be more confident,' her nan instructed her. 'Don't dab at the thing. Smooth it on like you're plastering a wall.'

'I've never plastered a wall.'

'What a sheltered life you've led.' Nan watched her in silence for a moment. 'Think about make-up, then. Like smoothing on your foundation for a girls' night out.'

'Haven't been on a girls' night out since my uni days,' Rosie muttered.

Her nan looked at, serious for once. 'Do you regret coming to live with an old bird like me? It's not too late to change your mind. I wouldn't kick up a fuss if you wanted to get a job in central London, and needed to move out. You know that, don't you?'

'Of course I don't regret it, Nan. What a silly thing to say.' Rosie hesitated, midway through icing the cake. 'Unless you want me to leave?'

'Now who's being silly?' Her nan chuckled. 'I've never had so much fun since you moved in. Nor had to do so much tidying up. In case your mum never mentioned this, underwear generally goes in drawers when clean and the wash basket when dirty. Not strewn all over the floor or hung from the lampshade.'

'Sorry.'

'But seriously, you're too young to be staying in every night, icing cakes and keeping an old lady company. You should be out, enjoying yourself before it's too late.'

'You make it sound like life ends at twenty-five.'

'It bloody well did for me,' her nan grumbled. 'It ended the day I got hitched to your grandfather, God rest his soul.'

Rosie looked at her sideways, frowning. 'God rest his soul? Grandad looked fine when I saw him last.'

'Eternal optimist, that's me. Old bastard must be due to drop dead any day now.'

Rosie raised her knife. 'Enough.'

'But you never date anyone, Rosie. Staying in every night, never bringing your friends round … It's not natural for a girl your age. I can't help but feel responsible. I'm not saying you should get married like I did, but you should be partying, enjoying yourself. Or occasionally dating at least. I mean, what if you forget how to …?' Her nan paused, then screwed up her face like she had eaten something sour. It was not a good look. 'You know …'

'No, I don't know.'

Nan rolled her eyes. 'Go on with you, you know perfectly well what I mean,' she said.

'No, I really don't. Forget how to … *what*?'

She nudged Rosie and whispered. 'Forget how to do it.'

Rosie stared, a little shocked. Though she ought not to be surprised. Her nan was always saying the most outrageous things.

'Maybe I can't forget. You can't forget what you've never learnt.'

Her nan gave her an old-fashioned look. 'Bit too late for that, young lady. I cleaned out your bedroom bin after the last time you came to stay. Virgins don't need pregnancy tests. Not unless you had a night-time visit from the blooming Archangel Gabriel.'

'You … ' Rosie gasped, then blushed darkly. 'That was a … a misunderstanding. And none of your business.'

'Just saying.'

'Well, you can just unsay it.' On impulse, she flicked the icing knife at her nan. 'Take that.'

A large blob of stiff, white, royal icing landed beside her nan's nose.

'Oh,' Nan said.

Rosie bit her lip in contrition. 'Sorry,' she apologised automatically, then some wicked inner demon made her flick the knife again. And again.

One new blob of icing hit her nan above the left eye. The other struck her on the chin, then dripped stickily to the kitchen floor.

'Oops,' she said innocently.

'Stop that.' Her nan stood motionless, staring at her with a dreadful look on her icing-dotted face. It was a look that meant vengeance would be coming soon. 'You're not too old to go over my knee, missy.'

'You and whose army?'

Her nan scooped a little icing out of the bowl, gazed

down at it speculatively for a few seconds, then flicked it towards Rosie.

It landed on her right cheek.

SPLAT.

'Why, you old … '

A knock at the front door to the flat surprised them into silence. They both turned, staring through the open kitchen door and down the narrow corridor that led to the front door.

'Who on earth … ?' Rosie muttered, then glanced at the clock on the wall. It was nearly nine o'clock in the evening. Hardly a good time for random visitors.

'Jehovah's Witnesses,' Nan offered, hurriedly reaching for a dishcloth to wipe her face, then added darkly, 'Though I didn't believe *they* would ever come back. Not after last time.'

'Maybe it's a neighbour, needing sugar or coffee.'

'None of my neighbours knock like that.'

Rosie knew what she meant. It had been a very business-like knock. An 'open this door right now and ask no questions' sort of knock. Like the Special Forces were at the door. Though of course the SAS would have blown it open and dropped black bags over their heads by now if that were the case.

She could not imagine any Special Forces wanting to kidnap her. Though her Nan was another matter; she was probably dabbling in industrial espionage on the dark net every night, instead of playing online Bingo like she claimed.

'Perhaps it's someone collecting for charity. And they're in a hurry.'

Nan raised her eyebrows steeply. 'They'll be in a hurry all right, when I send them away with a flea in their ear.'

The knock came again. Softer this time, more tentative.

'Carol singers?' Rosie suggested.

'Oh my goodness, yes,' Nan exclaimed, looking remorseful. 'It'll be that Mr Sinclair and his Heavenly

Christmas Choir, collecting in aid of PWD. The lady in the library told me they'd be coming round the flats one evening this week.'

'PWD?'

'Pets With Depression.' Nan threw down the sticky dishcloth and hurried away into the living room, saying over her shoulder, 'They were very good last year. You answer the door, love, tell them my favourite is *Good King Wenceslas*.' As she disappeared, she was already humming a snatch of the famous old carol under her breath. 'Give me a minute to find my purse.'

Smiling, the icing knife still in her hand, Rosie walked down to the front door of the flat and threw it open, expecting to find a group of shuffling, rosy-faced, hat-and-scarf-festooned carol singers outside on the landing.

Only it wasn't Mr Sinclair and his Heavenly Christmas Choir.

It was her boss.

CHAPTER SEVEN

He looked at the knife first.

'Expecting trouble?'

'Well, I wasn't expecting *you*,' she said bluntly, then remembered that she was speaking to her boss and forced herself to smile. Politely. With teeth showing. And a sticky blob of royal icing slowly stiffening on her right cheek.

She probably looked like a rabid dog.

Pyotr, on the other hand, looked more gorgeous than ever. And dressed up as though he had just come from the opera. Immaculate black tuxedo, bow tie and polished black shoes. He was holding his car keys in one hand, with a long, black, zip-up garment bag draped over the other arm.

'I mean, this is a surprise,' she added, completely flustered now. 'We thought you must be a Jehovah's Witness.'

Car keys jangling, he patted his suit pockets, then shook his head. 'Sorry, I'm all out of Watchtowers.' Then he straightened and looked pointedly at her cheek.

The one with the blob. 'Face pack? Make-up disaster?'

'I was icing a cake.'

'Don't get enough of that at work?'

'Oh, you know me, I live to ice,' she declared airily, and flourished the knife in the air.

A blob of icing landed on the lapel of his black suit jacket.

Pyotr looked down at it.

For a moment there was silence on the dimly-lit landing. The kind of anticipatory silence that makes your toes curl, she thought, and leaves even women with knives in their hands feeling very uncomfortable indeed.

Carefully, holding her breath, she leant forward and scraped the icing blob off the expensive lapel with the blade tip. He watched each glinting movement of the knife without saying a word.

'Sorry,' she whispered when it was all gone.

'No problem.'

'Would you like to come in?'

'Thank you.'

She stepped back and he entered the flat. 'I almost didn't recognise you,' she said, shutting the door after him, 'without your clothes on.'

'Come again?'

Rosie realised her mistake too late. Her face bloomed with heat like a ceramic hob. Now he was staring at her like she had two heads. Which would have been useful, she thought, because then she could have unscrewed the one that was blushing hotly and rammed it into the nearest bin.

'Whites,' she gabbled. 'Without your whites on, I mean.'

'I see,' he said drily, but did not take his gaze off her face. 'Look, I'm sure you must be wondering where I've come round here so late in the evening. Please believe me, I'm very sorry for the intrusion.'

'No, it's fine,' she lied.

'I wouldn't have come if it wasn't urgent.'

'This sounds serious.'

'It is.'

Rosie nodded. 'You'd better come into the living room, then.'

'Thank you,' he said again.

She held back, gesturing him to go first by pointing to the open door into the living room. 'Please,' she said, 'after you.'

He raised his brows, a touch of impatience in the dark eyes, but strode towards the living room without argument. He was on her territory now, she realised, and felt a little bolder. He might be her boss, but this was her home and he could not tell her what to do. She was in control of everything that happened here.

At that very moment, Nan came bustling out of the living room without looking, and the two of them collided.

'Ow, bloody hell,' her nan exclaimed, staring up at him in astonishment and rubbing her forehead, now smeared with traces of crumbly white icing. 'Who on earth are you?' She looked him up and down. 'And why do you look like a waiter? Nobody ordered Meals On Wheels.'

Pyotr, having recovered surprisingly quickly from their collision, tugged his crumpled jacket straight again and smiled. 'I'm Pyotr Wood,' he said, thrusting out a hand. 'I'm very pleased to meet you, and I apologise for the lateness of the hour. And for, erm, running into you. I run the bakery side of Minchin's Cake Shop. You must be … Rosie's grandmother?'

'That's right,' she agreed grudgingly, and shook his hand. 'I'm Nora. It's very nice to meet you at last, Mr … whatever-your-name-was. I was just looking for my purse. We thought you were carol singers.'

'Not a Jehovah's Witness, then?'

'Oh no, I threatened to take all my clothes off last time they knocked on the door. I don't think they'll be back.'

Pyotr frowned down at his hand as she dropped it. 'Have you been icing a cake too, by any chance?'

'Oops, yes, sorry about that. But never mind. You can wash your hands in the kitchen.' Nan took him by the arm and pushed him before her, leaving a few sticky fingerprints on the sleeve of his expensive-looking tuxedo jacket. 'This way, Peter.'

'Pyotr,' he corrected her.

'That's what I said, wasn't it?'

'No.'

'Well, if you're going to get all uppity about it … '

Rosie covered her face in shame.

In the kitchen, Pyotr eyed the marzipan-coated cake on the table, and the bowl of royal icing, and the flecks of icing everywhere, then made straight for the sink. A moment later his hands were clean and he was drying his hands on a dishcloth. Luckily, not the same one Nan had used to clean the icing off her face.

'Any chance we could talk alone?' he asked Rosie.

Nan rolled her eyes. 'Fine, fine, you two crack on. I know when I'm not wanted. I'll be in the living room. There's a smutty film on Channel Four in ten minutes. Might as well watch that with a box of Turkish Delight.'

'Thanks, Nan,' Rosie said helplessly.

Her nan pinched her arm on her way past. 'Now, girl, don't do anything I wouldn't. Which gives you pretty free rein.'

'Shh,' Rosie hissed.

'He's very sexy though. You didn't say he was sexy.' Nan looked back at Pyotr, and winked, much to Rosie's horror. 'I like a man who's not afraid to wear mascara.'

Then she disappeared.

Pyotr was still staring at the now closed door into the living room. 'What exactly,' he ventured, 'what did she mean by that?'

'Nothing.'

'She said … mascara.'

'Honestly, it's nothing. Ignore her. I'm going to be throttling her when you've gone, if it's any consolation.'

He glanced at himself in the reflective door of the microwave. 'It looks like I'm wearing mascara?'

'Long lashes.' She shook her head, not quite able to believe what she was saying. 'My nan is trying to say you have long lashes. For a man.'

He studied himself again, an expression of mild disdain on his face, then turned his head and looked at her instead. 'And how about you, Rosie?' His voice was like brandy cream over smoking hot Christmas pudding. 'What do you think?'

'I think … '

Her voice came out hoarse and choking, and Rosie had to stop and clear her throat. Twice. Noisily. Then grab a tumbler from the cupboard, pour herself some cold water from the tap, and down half the glassful in one quick inelegant gulp.

'Sorry,' she whispered, putting the glass down on the kitchen table and then pointing to herself, 'frog in my throat.'

His brows were raised. 'You were saying?'

'I was saying, I think you ought to tell me why you came here tonight.' She eyed the garment bag over his arm with misgiving. 'What's that?'

'A dress. For you.'

Her voice was a squeak of astonishment. Like a mouse being trodden on by a cruel foot. *'For me?'*

'You see,' Pyotr murmured, holding her gaze as though his eyes were pure magnet, 'I need a woman.'

Her own eyes widened. Along with her mouth. Not a very ladylike expression. That invisible foot applied yet more pressure to the mouse. 'You need a … a … *woman?*'

'More specifically, Rosie,' he continued smoothly, 'I need *you.*'

Pyotr thought he had gone too far with that.

He watched her eyes widen, two electric-blue sea anemones ringed with stubby lashes, and her heart-shaped face grow pale, her lips parting so invitingly in surprise that it was all he could do not to lean forward and press a kiss on them.

He felt his groin stiffen, and cursed silently. If only he knew more women on a casual basis, women he could have asked to do this favour for him, women he did not so badly want to take to bed. But he had been careful to keep himself aloof since returning to London, his only contacts those he had known in the past. So he had found himself in a desperate situation tonight, and had known instinctively that Rosie Redpath was the only woman he knew who could be relied upon to help him.

Yes, she was the woman he needed.

'What for?' she asked, and now he could see suspicion in her eyes. 'I can't work late. Not tonight. It's been too long a day.'

'This isn't about work.'

Rosie stared. 'I don't understand … '

'I need you to accompany me to a party. Tonight. Right now, in fact. It's urgent, otherwise I wouldn't ask.'

'Thanks.' There was resentment in her tone, and he realised too late that she had taken his words the wrong way. 'All your usual dates cried off, did they?'

Her grandmother interrupted with, 'It's rather late for a date, isn't it?'

To his relief, Rosie turned and bustled the old lady out of the kitchen, whispering something fiercely that he did not quite catch. Then the door closed on her grandmother's curious stare, and they were alone together.

Pyotr closed his eyes, mentally composing himself. When he opened them again, he found her standing in front of him, a perplexed frown on her face.

He guessed that he must be behaving erratically, at least from her point of view. As a boss, he had always tried to be a steady presence in the bakery, keeping a strict eye on production values and making sure the employees could come to him with any problems. Now he had shown up at her door, late in the evening, dressed unusually, and with a very odd proposition. No wonder she was still looking suspicious.

'Sorry, allow me to start again.' He managed to smile at her, and not sound quite so strained. 'Rosie, I would be honoured if you would accompany me to a party tonight.'

'Where?'

He hesitated. 'Mayfair.' He saw her eyebrows shoot up at the mention of such an expensive area of London, known worldwide as the playground of the rich and famous, and added, 'The party is being held at the home of an old friend of mine.'

'Know a lot of billionaires, do you?'

He shrugged, a little uncomfortable with pursuing that.

'So what's his name, this friend of yours?'

'He is a she,' he said quietly. 'Natalya.'

Her eyes widened again. 'Russian, by any chance?'

Pyotr nodded.

'An old flame, I'm guessing. And you want this … Natalya to think you're over her. That you've moved on. Am I right?'

He hesitated again, then nodded slowly. 'Very astute of you.' He could not have thought of a more perfect reason if he had spent days fabricating an elaborate cover story. 'Will you do it?'

'A glamorous party in Mayfair, on the arm of a drop-dead gorgeous male in a very expensive tuxedo – don't get anything on that tux, by the way; the hire companies charge a fortune for damage – now let me see …' Rosie cast her eyes up to the striplight on the white-washed kitchen ceiling, then looked back at him ironically. 'Why yes, I might just possibly be interested. Though, you know, spending the next hour slapping a ton of royal icing on my nan's Christmas cake is still running a very close second.'

'Good,' he said, relieved.

'There's only one problem, in fact.'

'Which is what?'

Looking depressed, Rosie indicated her stained apron and the tatty jeans and jumper underneath. 'I don't have a single glamorous thing to wear. Not a stitch. Remember Cinderella? I expect she had more in her closet than I do.'

'That's no problem; I already thought of that.' He smiled, and held out the black garment bag. 'You shall go to the ball, Cinders.'

Rosie stared at the garment bag. 'Is that … a … dress? For … me?' When he nodded, suspicion flared in her eyes again. 'Oh no, sorry. I couldn't possibly accept such an expensive gift.'

'It goes back to the hire shop tomorrow,' he promised her, lying blithely. In fact he had bought it specially. But he knew she would slap him down if she knew that. To her, he was only the partner in a small bakery and catering firm, and that kind of expense might suggest some rather unpleasant motivations. 'So don't get any of that icing on it, okay?'

She took the garment bag, looked bewildered. 'But my size … I don't understand. How could you be sure … '

Pyotr smiled at her naivety. He looked her up and down assessingly, admiring her slim waist and pleasing curves at hip and breast. 'Don't worry, I've got a fairly good eye for that kind of thing.'

'I bet,' she replied, rather sharply, and now there was a faint flush in her cheeks.

He nodded towards the door. 'Grab a quick shower, put the dress on, tights and heels, make-up, jewellery, the works. I'll wait.' He glanced at his watch. 'Shall we say thirty minutes?'

Halfway out of the kitchen door, Rosie glared back at him. 'Thirty minutes? Shall we say you're delusional?'

'Forty-five, then.' He picked a stiff piece of icing off the edge of the bowl and tasted it. Not bad. He ought to get her icing the next batch of Christmas cakes next week. 'Come on, Rosie. We need to be at the party for eleven o'clock at the latest.'

When she did not move, Pyotr turned to find her still glaring at him, a peremptory hand on her hip, the garment bag slung over one shoulder. 'Please,' he added softly, and smiled when she muttered, 'Harumph,' under her breath and stalked off with her new dress.

As soon as he was alone, his smile faded.

Was he going mad?

Or had he finally lost his sense of morality?

Bad enough that he was dragging another person into the surreal drama that was his life, but that Rosie was clearly innocent and inexperienced, not to mention under his immediate supervision at work, made the decision almost criminal.

But he would not have come here tonight if he had not been desperate.

This could be his only chance to speak to Natalya, and it would have been too difficult to crash the party stag. No, taking a date had been his best option if he wanted to get past the heavies on the door.

A little voice in his head mocked his excuses, whispering. 'You want that woman in your bed.' But he ignored it.

There was more at stake here than the risk of getting his cover blown.

So to speak.

CHAPTER EIGHT

Rosie could hardly believe her eyes. 'It's like being in a fairy tale,' she whispered, gazing around herself as she stepped out of the taxi, her stiletto heels clacking on the pavement.

Christmas lights were everywhere in central London, rope upon festive rope of them, glittering and shining and winking above shoppers in the icy wind. Down some of the shopping streets, she had glimpsed huge gold and white stars hung suspended alongside red and green baubles, while glorious, green-branched Christmas trees, decorated with tinsel and silver-wrapped chocolates and yet more dancing lights, seemed to be in every shop window.

And here she was now, wearing a silver sheath dress so tight and slick to the touch it could have been snakeskin, with a plunge neckline, no sleeves, and a hemline so short she was worried that if she bent over inadvertently, Her Majesty's Constabulary would be summoned.

Like a naughty erotic version of Cinderella, she thought, gazing down at herself in wonder. Minus the pumpkins.

'Wish I'd brought a cardigan,' she muttered, shivering as flakes of snow skidded past on the breeze. The dress had a bolero jacket with it, but the sleeves only came to mid-elbow, and it was fairly skimpy.

Beside her, Pyotr was paying the driver who had driven them through busy streets into central London. She could not begin to imagine the expense. But Pyotr had not blinked at the sum on the driver's clock, merely reached into an inner pocket of his divine tuxedo and brought out a supple leather wallet.

'Ready?'

'To be eaten by a fairy tale monster?' she quipped. 'Why not? As long as the frog turns into a prince at the end of the night.'

He raised his brows, clearly bemused. 'Did I miss something?'

'Only most of the journey here.'

'Yes, sorry about that.' He checked his phone for the hundredth time, then slipped it apologetically into that inner pocket along with his wallet. 'I was hoping for a call. But no luck so far.'

She hesitated. 'You have been invited to this party, haven't you?'

'Of course,' he said smoothly, then added, 'in a manner of speaking.'

She stared.

'Come on.' Pyotr put an arm about her waist and led her down the street to one of the more expensive-looking buildings, all white stucco and pillars and gleaming steps. 'Stop looking so nervous. I want you to enjoy yourself.'

'Are the party guests all going to be Russian?'

'Not all of them,' he demurred.

'Embassy staff?' She glanced at the burly black limousine with darkened windows and what she guessed must be an embassy crest on the door panel.

'Probably a few,' he admitted.

She stopped dead. 'Wait, I can't do this. Sorry.'

'What's the matter?' Pyotr demanded, looking at her with dark eyes. She might have described them as wild if she had been an imaginative person. But being a touch prosaic, she merely wondered if he was going down with a cold. There was impatience in his brusque tone as he continued, 'Look, Rosie, I need you to trust me. I admit, it's true that I wasn't officially invited to this party. But I know these people and they're not going to turn me away, especially with you on my arm.'

'No, I mean, I genuinely can't do this. I'm stuck.' She pointed to the slim black heel of her stiletto, which had become lodged in a narrow crack in the pavement. 'Sorry, could you possibly … ?'

'I see.'

Pyotr grinned at her predicament; not a very gentlemanlike response, she thought, pursing her lips. But he bent at once to release her, one hand clasped warmly about her bare ankle.

At his touch, she felt heat rise in her body. Blimey, she thought. Just as well Pyotr had no idea how she felt about him, otherwise he would almost certainly be pressing his advantage here. And that wouldn't be the only thing he would be pressing, she considered darkly.

'There you go,' he murmured, releasing her stiletto.

'Thanks.'

He led her up the white steps and through the front door, which was standing ajar. Just inside was a burly man in a dark suit who held up a hand.

'Sorry, sir, madam, private party,' he told them, his accent decidedly foreign.

'I know, that's why we're here.'

'Invitations?'

Pyotr ran a hand through his dark hair, looking at the man impatiently. 'Here's the thing. I've come here straight from dinner and the theatre. And I forgot to ask my secretary to put the invitations in my jacket pocket.'

The big man in the suit shook his head, his mouth compressed, his chunky face unmoved. There was sweat lining his forehead, presumably due to the overhead heater that was pumping out hot air towards the doorway. His eyes looked like two black currants sunk into unbaked dough. Rosie tried not to imagine the size of the oven required to bake that particular delicacy.

'No invitation, no entry,' he told them flatly.

Rosie shivered theatrically, rubbing her arms. 'Brr,' she muttered, 'it's freezing out here.' But the doorman paid no attention whatsoever.

'Are you going to cause me hassle?' Pyotr asked, looking the man up and down. He slipped a hand casually inside his trouser pocket, standing there with apparent nonchalance, looking almost exactly like a male model in his black tuxedo. 'Because that would be unwise of you.'

'Give us a minute, would you?' Rosie asked the man, shooting him what she hoped was her most dazzling smile.

The doorman shrugged.

She turned her back on him, glaring at Pyotr. 'When you said you hadn't officially been invited, I thought you were exaggerating,' she whispered, leaning in close. Gosh, his aftershave was alluring! She avoided staring at his broad chest under the smooth black jacket. He looked like James Bond tonight, all rugged and muscular sex appeal in a tux, and it was making her forget things. Like the fact that she was angry. Damn him. 'I thought there might be an awkward moment when we got spotted by the hostess. I didn't know there would be a bouncer on the door.'

'These are embassy people. They probably have security everywhere.'

'This is embarrassing.'

His smile was thin. 'I'm going to get us in. Just leave this to me.'

'Then do your thing. Or I shall,' she warned him.

Pyotr met her gaze with a hard look of his own. 'I've got this, okay?'

'Let's see it, then.'

'Look, I don't want to interrupt, but I suggest you both turn around and leave.' The large man sounded bored. 'No more of this ... whispering.'

Pyotr raised his eyebrows, gazing at him over her shoulder with a look of pitying disdain. '*Whee-spring?*'

Rosie turned, keeping close to Pyotr. She felt a little intimidated now. The man's face had tightened, like someone kneading the dough, and his eye-currants were all bunched up now. It was slightly nauseating to watch.

He wagged a sturdy finger at them both. His trigger finger, she could not help thinking. 'Don't make fun of my English,' he warned them. 'Or I break your arms. All four of them.'

Shocked, Rosie thrust both hands behind her back, keeping a tight hold on her clutch purse. 'Excuse me? You're not breaking my arms, mate.'

What was that accent, Rosie wondered? Russian? There were a few Russian families in the block of flats where she and her nan lived, and they did sound vaguely similar. But wherever he came from, he did not seem like a very pleasant or accommodating doorman.

The man picked up a walkie-talkie from the hall table and showed it to them, his smile cold. 'Outside. Now. Don't make me call for back-up.'

The situation was not promising.

Damn it, she thought crossly, I came here to party.

Rosie looked up the broad flight of stairs to where a noisy party was taking place on the first floor. The whole place was decked out with gorgeous Christmas decorations, large and very expensive-looking baubles and lights and tinsel everywhere. She could see dozens of glamorous people wandering about rather drunkenly under the chandeliers, champagne flutes in hand.

Impulsively, she raised a hand and waved to one of them, then called out, 'Cooey! Is that you, erm ... Sonya?' That was the only Russian-sounding woman's name she could think of on the spot. 'How lovely to see you again.'

Pyotr turned his head to stare at her in a bemused and annoyed fashion. 'What on earth do you think you're doing?' he demanded through gritted teeth, keeping his voice at a low enough level that the big lug stopping them from crashing this party could not possibly hear him.

'Shut up and play along,' she hissed back.

One of the women upstairs paused near the head of the

stairs and peered down at her uncertainly. She was a willowy redhead in a fabulous, figure-hugging green dress with matching heels, her lipstick almost the same shade as her hair.

'Sonya, it's me, Rosie!' she continued blithely, waving her hand for all she was worth and hoping the woman was not actually called Sonya. That would be awkward. Her bracelets jangled together, and more heads turned upstairs. Several other people drifted to the head of the stairs to stare down at them in the hall.

'Merry Christmas!' Rosie called again, rather pleased to see that she had attracted a small audience, then laughed. 'So silly of us, we seem to have forgotten our invitations.'

The redhead came halfway down the stairs. 'Karl?'

'Madam?' the burly doorman said respectfully, turning towards the woman at once, though it was clear he did not want to take his eyes off them.

'Let them come upstairs.'

The currants jogged up and down on the spot, then froze beneath stern black brows. 'Yes, madam,' he agreed reluctantly, and stepped back. He gave them a look of acute dislike. 'You may go upstairs.'

Rosie glanced triumphantly at Pyotr as they headed for the stairs, and surprised a tense look on his face. Had she embarrassed him with her little party-crashing ruse? The thought was a little unnerving. But at least she had managed to get their foot in the door, which was more than he had done, fabulous tuxedo or not.

The redhead met them halfway. She dismissed Rosie with barely a glance, then fixed Pyotr with a long, cool smile.

'Pyotr,' she said in a husky voice, leaving Rosie in no doubt that these two knew each other. And intimately too, by the generous way the redhead kissed him on each cheek, then on the lips for good measure, her hand lingering on his shoulder as she drew back. 'How are you? It's been years.'

'I was in America.'

'Ah yes, your precious America. And now you turn up here unannounced.' Again she swept Rosie with a cursory glance. 'I did not think you liked your women that young. Or unsophisticated.'

'Erm, excuse me? I'm standing right here,' Rosie pointed out bluntly.

Pyotr shot her a quelling look, then murmured something in what she presumed was his native tongue. Russian. She had no idea what he was saying to the redhead; to her, it sounded close to something the Muppet Chef might have gurgled while juggling rubber chickens. But she could not mistake the interest in his smouldering gaze, damn him.

His gaze dwelt first on the redhead's low and annoyingly ample cleavage, then moved down to her long legs and shapely ankles in the shimmering green heels. Pyotr found this woman attractive, she realised, clenching her fists instinctively. Though it was true that probably ninety percent of the male heterosexual population would find a woman like that attractive, and also that she was not with him on a real 'date' but just as a favour, Rosie still did not enjoy watching his gaze move over the redhead's lithe, slim-hipped figure like he was planning on getting reacquainted with it later.

The redhead replied with the same guttural tones, rolling her 'r's in what appeared to be passionate disagreement, then placed a hand on his chest.

Pyotr covered her hand with his own, muttering something under his breath while staring into the other woman's almond-shaped eyes.

By then, Rosie had had enough of this reunion. She cleared her throat noisily. 'Sorry to interrupt, but do I need to be here for this conversation?'

'Forgive me, I forgot for a moment that you do not speak Russian. Natalya and I were just catching up.' Pyotr turned to her, his dark eyes unreadable. He held out his arm. 'Shall we go upstairs?'

Rosie hesitated, then reluctantly rested her hand on his black sleeve. 'Thank you,' she said, a little ungraciously.

The redhead – Natalya, presumably – stepped aside for them to continue up the stairs, but her smile was mocking.

'After you,' she said in English, 'please.'

Upstairs, the stately, high-ceilinged rooms were thronging with party-goers. Gold tinsel and tasteful faux green garlands were festooned around the large, gilt mirrors and picture frames, and above doorways. Everyone was very glamorous. Her own fancy sheath dress quite paled in comparison, she realised with a sinking feeling. Most of the women guests appeared to be wearing designer gear, the kind of outrageously expensive and impractical clobber she had only ever been able to gawp at in the pages of Vogue. Silk scarves disguised as dresses, bizarre one-sleeved tunics, and cardigans with buttons and no discernible holes.

Even the waitresses holding trays of champagne flutes looked more glamorous than her.

'Are you all right?' Pyotr asked, looking at her.

She realised then that she had stopped dead next to him, staring around at their glittering surroundings. 'Suddenly I feel like Cinderella. And any minute my coach is going to turn back into a pumpkin, and you … ' She looked him up and down speculatively. 'You'll be a mouse running about my kitchen.'

'A large mouse, I hope.'

'The biggest on the block,' she stated.

The redhead had come up behind them and must have heard this exchange. She was staring from Rosie to Pyotr, a slight frown on her flawless face.

'Pyotr, you are … mouse?' she repeated, clearly bemused.

'But a big one,' he agreed.

'Bloody enormous, in fact,' Rosie said, then added

under her breath, a little crossly, 'With huge sooty whiskers. More like a rat than a mouse, actually. A great, smelly rat down a sewer.'

Pyotr raised his eyebrows at her and she fell silent.

'Darling, will you not introduce me to your … interesting friend?' the redhead purred, her fake smile revealing perfectly even white teeth. Not bad for the wrong side of thirty, Rosie thought, but smiled back. Perhaps the woman was married. With five children. But she doubted it.

'Natalya, this is Rosie Redpath. We work together.'

This time it was the redhead's turn to raise her eyebrows. 'You work together?'

He hesitated. 'At a bakery.'

Natalya stared at him, then threw back her head and laughed as though he had said something truly hilarious. 'How amusing you are, Pyotr. Now the truth, please.'

'That is the truth,' Rosie said stiffly.

The woman swivelled her gaze mechanically towards Rosie as though her eyeballs were made of glass. Which would have been a relief. No one could be so perfect and not have something fake about them, she thought, and then told herself off for being so uncharitable.

'No,' she said coldly. 'I do not believe it.'

Pyotr slipped a proprietorial arm about Rosie's waist and drew her nearer, as though to demonstrate that she was under his protection. Either that or he had spotted the flushed look on her face, which probably told him she was close to poking this woman in the nose.

'Rosie, this is Natalya. An old friend of mine.'

Rosie smiled grimly at the redhead. 'How do you do?'

'Hmm,' was all Natalya seemed able to manage.

He looked from Rosie to the other woman without saying anything, but his arm tightened almost imperceptibly about her waist.

'So, tell me, how do you two know each other?' Rosie asked, snatching a flute of champagne off a passing tray and gulping down a sweet, sharp, bubbly mouthful.

'We were lovers once,' Natalya stated boldly at the exact same time as Pyotr muttered, 'She was at college with my sister.'

Rosie felt very hot and flustered. And not just because the temperature upstairs was much higher than it had been on the street.

'Oh.'

Pyotr closed his eyes briefly, then released her waist. 'Rosie, I know this is a great deal to ask of you, but ... I need to speak to Natalya alone. Will you be all right waiting here for me?'

She looked at him and saw again that mental image of the rat with great, sooty-black whiskers. but she nodded and smiled with artificial brightness. 'Of course,' she said loudly. 'I'm sure the two of you must have a lot of catching up to do.'

'Ten minutes,' he promised her huskily. 'No more.'

She took another gulp of champagne and felt the bubbles tickling her nose. 'Go, I'll be fine. Don't worry about me,' she insisted, then watched as he nodded to Natalya and the two of them walked swiftly away into a side room and closed the door.

Her voice dropped to a fierce mutter. 'When you come back I'll be dancing the Tarantella on the buffet table with nothing on. But   I'm sure you won't even notice, you stinky, Russian love rat.'

'Excuse me?'

She spun, forgetting her high heels, and would probably have ended up taking a dive into the old couple in front of her if a hand had not caught her elbow.

'Steady,' a male voice said, sounding amused.

'Oh crap,' Rosie swore, having managed to spill the last of her champagne on her dress. She dashed it away with the back of her hand. 'Sorry, I'm so bloody clumsy. Did I get any on you?'

'Not a drop, I assure you.'

She looked up and straightened in surprise. It was a man about her own age, slim and undeniably attractive in a black tuxedo, dark-haired like Pyotr but with dancing eyes and a light smile on his lips.

'Hello,' she breathed, clutching her empty flute glass. 'Who are you?'

'Grigori,' he said with great charm, and inclined his head. 'At your service. Now, what were you saying about dancing the Tarantella with no clothes on? I would very much like to see that.'

CHAPTER NINE

The room into which Pyotr had been shown was illuminated only by soft uplighters on the walls, but even in that dim light he could sense the opulence of his surroundings. A red and gold daybed dominated the room against the far wall, its back of ornate dark wood, its legs polished and shining. Above it hung a portrait of some elderly Russian diplomat from the Victorian era, stern in his embroidered cap and grey curly beard; he had known the man's name once, now it escaped him. On one side of the daybed stood a six-foot-high mahogany cabinet with double doors, gleaming with beauty. On its other side, there was a more discreet occasional table. It boasted exquisite mother-of-pearl inlay in an hexagonal pattern, on top of which stood a collection of vodka bottles, a silver cocktail shaker, ice bucket and a tray of metal-encased glasses, some of which were still partly full.

Natalya kicked off her heels and trod barefoot across the hand-made Persian rug to the mother-of-pearl table.

'Would you like a Black Russian?' she asked, her voice alluringly husky. 'Unless you would prefer champagne?'

'Black Russian would be great, thank you.'

He replied instinctively in Russian, slipping back into

his mother tongue with ease. Literally his *mother's* tongue. For though he had been born in London and partially brought up here, his Russian heritage was not something he would ever lose, having lived in Russia during his student days, and learned their old folk tales and songs as a child on his mother's knee.

He studied Natalya's back as she poured five parts of vodka into two glasses over ice, then gently added two parts coffee liqueur. The intoxicating smell of the cocktail soon filled the room, and he wondered if he should have refused to drink with her. She had not changed much physically. A few lines on her face that had not been there before, and her breasts were fuller. But she seemed to him as lithe and seductive as ever, which was undoubtedly why she was still so influential in international circles.

The woman was beautiful, yes. But deadly too. He had not forgotten what had happened last time they had met. It had been a mistake on his part, trusting her.

He would not make that mistake again. But she could still be useful.

'There. That should warm you up after tonight's snow.' Natalya turned to him with a flickering smile, handing him a Black Russian and then sipping at her own. Her eyes watched him closely. 'Shall we sit?'

Pyotr looked about. There was nowhere to sit in the room except on the opulent daybed. Together.

Reluctantly he sat down. She took a long, deep swallow of her Black Russian, then somehow managed to drape herself over him without their bodies actually touching. Her arm along the ornate wooden back of the daybed was close enough to make the hairs tingle on the nape of his neck though.

'Oh Pyotr,' she purred. 'It is so marvellous to see you again. It is almost like the old days in Moscow. But who is that girl with you? And what is this talk of a ... a bakery?'

'Just something I'm doing at the moment,' he said curtly, not wishing to give too much away. 'It was necessary.'

She nodded, accepting that calmly. But then she had probably done a few similar things in her time. Her hand made contact, brushing the short hair at the back of his head. 'And the girl ?'

He resisted the urge to move away. He knew Natalya; she was mercenary, she would give him nothing without something in return. But her touch made him uncomfortable. Like sitting still while a python draped its heavy coils about him.

'I told you, a colleague.'

'You are sleeping with her?'

'No.'

She smiled slowly, watching him. 'But soon.'

'I told you, no.'

'Oh please.' She sounded partly offended, partly amused. 'Do not insult my intelligence by attempting to deny it. I am not a fool and I have been in your bed myself.' Her tone sharpened. 'I saw the way you looked at her, my old friend. Like a starving man looking at a hot meal.'

He shrugged, trying to sound casual. 'She is attractive, that is all.'

'Yes, and any attractive woman will soon find her way into your bed.' Her fingers began to stroke his neck, rhythmic, insistent. 'But how could it be otherwise? You are a very sexy man, Pyotr. And the girl is clearly panting for you.'

He sipped his Black Russian. It was divine.

'You think so?'

She laughed. 'I am a woman. Trust me, she wants you. Like I want you.'

'Don't be ridiculous.'

'Nothing has changed, Pyotr. Oh yes, we are both a little older. But the old chemistry is still here.' She stroked his cheek, and he half-turned his head, looking into sultry eyes smokily outlined in black kohl. 'One kiss, and you would be mine again.'

'Don't be so sure. I haven't forgotten Moscow.'

Her red lips curved in a satisfied smile. 'I knew you could not have done. But you are too unfair. What happened was not my fault. How was I to know Boris would come home from Paris so early?'

'You didn't even tell me you were married.'

'I'm not.' She made a face. 'Not any more. Poor, dear Boris.'

'Dead?'

'Fell from a high window. It was very sad.'

'So now you're the grieving widow?'

'Believe me, I have no pockets in this dress, it would spoil the lines. But I am never usually without a handkerchief.'

He took another sip of Black Russian. The vodka bit into his bloodstream, the coffee liqueur thick and darkly nutty and bitter-sweet as love. He swore silently to himself, lowering the metal-encased glass. The heady combination of tastes, and the alcohol rushing through his system, was leaving him dangerously open to suggestion. Memories of childhood flashed through him, rich and intense, and it was all he could do to avoid being taken over by them, to avoid relaxing in Natalya's seductive company and forgetting why he had come, and the young woman waiting outside for him.

Rosie Redpath.

The homely British name worked on him like a charm, snapping him out of his dark and brooding reverie.

Rosie Redpath. She had come here tonight without any agenda and without asking any difficult questions. And she was relying on him not to leave her stranded in a party full of strangers.

Pyotr balanced the glass precariously on the wooden arm of the daybed. 'Thank you for the cocktail, Natalya. It's delicious. But I did not come here to talk about the old days.'

She shrugged delicately, waiting and watching.

'I came to ask you a favour,' he admitted, and saw nothing in her face. 'Will you help me?'

'I don't do favours.'

He met her gaze. 'For the sake of my sister. Do not pretend you have forgotten her. The two of you were close once.'

Something flickered in her cold, beautiful face. 'Of course I have not forgotten Irina. What happened to her was a tragedy. But your sister is long dead. I do not see how this can be connected to – '

'Her young daughter was with her when she and Nikolai were murdered. The girl was never found.'

'So?' Natalya shrugged again, more aggressively. 'That was years ago. The child is either dead or gone forever by now. Besides, the police said there was no evidence that they even had their daughter with them that night. Nikolai was not a fool; he knew there might be trouble. Surely he would have sent the child away for her own safety?' She made a small, fatalistic gesture. 'She was probably staying with friends the night they were killed. Friends who later sent the child home to Russia.'

'And failed to tell anyone in the family where she was?'

Her eyes flashed. 'Not everyone in your family is to be trusted, Pyotr,' she said bitterly. 'And as I recall, you were in America with your parents when it happened. Perhaps Irina's friends thought the girl would be better off being brought up by someone outside the family.'

He felt a stirring of suspicion at her certainty. 'Do you know more than you're telling? Was the child with you that night?'

She looked shocked. 'Of course not. Good God, who would have been crazy enough to give me a child of four years old to look after? Besides, you are forgetting, I was not in London that year. I was still in Moscow in those days, barely much more than a child myself.'

He closed his eyes. 'Natalya, I have to find her.'

'Why?'

'Anastasiya is my niece. I owe it to my sister to keep looking for her.'

'Your loyalty to your dead sister is so touching. A pity your loyalty to the living is less powerful.'

Natalya put a warm hand on his thigh, stroking him suggestively, and he opened his eyes, turning his head to stare into her disturbing eyes.

'For the past year, since I came back to London after hearing that Anastasiya might be here, I have had detectives looking for the girl. Rumours and whispers, false sightings, cold trails … And finally, I have a lead that feels like the real thing.' He sighed. 'But even if it is my niece, I may never get a chance to see her before she disappears again. The child is protected and I cannot get near her.'

'So you came to me for help,' she said simply.

'You know our people in London. You are influential. And more than that, you know those involved.'

Her eyes widened. The hand stopped stroking. 'Who do you mean?'

He named a family whose dangerous reputation was known to most Russians on London. And to the British authorities too, he was certain of it.

She sat up straight, all pretence at seduction gone. 'You must be mad.'

'Far from it.'

'I am telling you as a friend, Pyotr, you had better give up this insanity now. Even to think of intervening with such people would be suicidal.'

'Let me worry about that.'

'I am not thinking about you. You should never have come here. If they took the girl into their own family after what happened to Irina and Nikolai, you can be sure it was not out of goodwill, but as security. Which means they will know who you are, and your relationship to the child.' She shuddered. 'My God, one of that family is out there tonight, enjoying our hospitality. If they were to find out what I have been discussing with you … '

Hope raced through him. One of them was here tonight?

Pyotr stood up, glancing at the closed door. Suddenly he remembered Rosie. She was still out there, alone and undefended, ignorant of the true reason for their visit. If she were to say something in her usual, unguarded way …

'Which one?' he demanded urgently. 'Quick, give me a name.'

Rosie laughed uproariously at the end of Grigori's anecdote, then grabbed another handful of caviar and soured cream blinis from a passing waiter, who gave her a disdainful glance but said nothing. She kept looking to her right and wishing Pyotr would reappear from the side room into which he had vanished with the vampish Natalya a good forty minutes ago. But although Grigori was no substitute for her boss, being a little too smooth for her tastes, he was both good-looking and flatteringly attentive, and he did at least tell very funny stories.

'Mmm, these are delicious. So, did they ever find out who stole their clothes line?'

'Never.'

'You must have been quite a devil.'

'Not at all,' he insisted, grinning. 'I was a bored seven-year-old with time on my hands. And those women deserved what they got.'

'Nowhere to hang their damp knickers?'

Grigori smiled, and inclined his sleek dark head. 'Precisely.' He drained his champagne flute, then studied her thoughtfully. 'So you say that you make Christmas cakes for a living.'

'All sorts of cakes,' she corrected him, 'though Christmas is just around the corner, so yes, at the moment I do tend to be rolling out the marzipan rather frequently.'

'With the man who accompanied you here tonight?'

'My boss, Pyotr.'

Grigori nodded, his gaze on her face. He was still smiling, but for some reason she felt suddenly uneasy. 'A good Russian name.'

'As opposed to a bad Russian name?' Rosie joked, then fell silent when he did not laugh with her. 'Sorry. I didn't mean to be rude. Me and my stupid tongue. My nan says I shouldn't be allowed out, I'm always saying the wrong thing.'

'Or maybe the right thing, but to the wrong person,' a voice said behind her.

It was Pyotr.

She had never been so pleased to have a man creep up behind her in her life. 'Oh, you're back,' she gabbled, turning to smile at him, and then saw how cold and hard his eyes were, staring over her shoulder at Grigori. 'This is – '

'I know who this is,' Pyotr interrupted.

Grigori nodded. 'Good evening, Pyotr. I must admit, when I saw you walk in here tonight with this charming young lady, I was surprised. I did not even know you were in London.'

'I've been keeping a low profile.'

'As a baker, I believe.'

Pyotr stiffened, and then shot an accusing look at Rosie.

'Is it a secret?' she demanded, a little flushed now. 'Well, I'm sorry, but perhaps you should have told me that before sneaking off with the Bond girl lookalike.'

'I did not sneak,' he told her coldly.

'Oh, pardon me, I must have meant *crawled off*. Like a rat!' She threw her hands wide in a gesture of bewildered annoyance. The last dregs of champagne in her glass flew wide and hit him in the eye. 'Oops.'

The tall Russian woman was standing behind him, listening to their exchange with disbelief. She crooked a dark enquiring brow at Rosie. '*Bond girl?*'

Pyotr, wiping the champagne from his eye, shook his head. 'I believe she means a female Russian spy from one of the Bond films.'

'Yes,' Rosie agreed thankfully, gesturing with her champagne glass again, and only belatedly realising how crazy she must sound, 'yes, that's exactly what … I … what I meant.'

Sighing, Pyotr took the glass away from her and placed it on the half-empty tray of a nearby waiter. 'Can I get you another drink?' he asked her politely enough. When Rosie shook her head, he looked relieved, and then turned to the Russian woman. 'Natalya? Some more champagne?'

'Thank you, darling.'

He took two full champagne flutes from the tray, gave one to Natalya and kept the other for himself, then suddenly, without any warning, threw the contents of his glass full into Grigori's face.

Taken by surprise, Grigori staggered back, his face dripping. 'What the hell … ?' he demanded thickly.

Pyotr looked back at him without flinching, the flute dangling from his hand. 'Oops,' he said calmly, in an echo of Rosie's exclamation.

'Are you mad?'

'No,' Pyotr told him. 'In fact, I'm just coming to my senses.' He took Rosie's hand, shaking his head at Grigori's wild, blinking glance about the crowded room. 'Don't bother calling your heavies to throw us out, we're leaving anyway. Meanwhile, I suggest you have a talk with Natalya. She knows what I want – and what I intend to do if I don't get it.'

As they made hurriedly for the stairs, Rosie snatched a flaky pastry mince pie from a buffet table in passing. 'Sorry,' she told the portly lady next to the table, who was wearing what looked like a real mink wrap and staring after them both in amazement, 'I'm addicted to mince pies. I have to eat one every quarter of an hour or I get sick. It's a rare seasonal condition, very rare,' she called incorrigibly over her shoulder as Pyotr dragged her away. 'Only one in a million people suffer from it at Christmas. It's called Mincemania.'

Outside in the cold, Pyotr pulled her after him for several dark, icy blocks, ignoring her squeals of protest as her high heels skidded in the snowy streets.

'What on earth is going on?' she demanded breathlessly.

Pyotr looked behind them, then slowed his pace at last, seemingly satisfied that they were not being followed. 'I can't tell you.'

'Oh, for goodness' sake!'

'Not here, at least. Perhaps somewhere more private.' He shot her a serious look. 'If you're sure you want to know the truth about me, that is. It's not a very savoury tale, I'm afraid.'

'That's okay, I prefer sweet to savoury,' she declared airily.

He stared, his hand tightening on hers. Then suddenly he whisked her sideways, down a dark alley to their right, the narrow space cluttered with commercial skips and black bin bags awaiting collection, the ground underfoot slushy and cold.

'What are you doing? Pyotr?' She gasped as he pushed her up against the brick wall, the cold striking into her body.

'Something I've been wanting to do for a long time,' he said huskily.

Oh my God, she thought with a sudden shock, he's a killer. A Russian assassin. And she was his next victim.

'Don't try it, mate,' she said, threatening him with her mince pie. 'I'm armed.'

His gaze, wry and amused, flickered from her face to her fingers curled about the raised mince pie. 'Flaky or shortcrust?'

'Flaky, of course.'

'They're always the tastiest. Shame to waste it on me.'

'I can live with the loss.'

'Better let me have it, then. Just not in the face, okay?'

Rosie stared, then slowly lowered the mince pie. It was a bit crushed now, anyway. Bits of mincemeat were clinging to her fingers, sweet and sticky. 'You didn't bring me down here to kill me, did you?'

'Why on earth would you think something like that?'

'Your behaviour back there ... '

'I threw a glass of wine in an enemy's face. I didn't shoot him.'

'But you wanted to?'

'No. I told you, I'm not a killer. I just wanted to show Grigori I was serious.'

She took a shaky breath. 'Why are we here, then?'

Pyotr stroked her hair away from her cheek. His heavy lids lifted to meet her gaze, and his eyes glinted in the darkness. 'I think you know why I brought you down here, Rosie Redpath.'

'Oh no,' she whispered. 'No, no ... '

'Yes,' he insisted, then leant slowly forward, as though giving her ample time to escape, and kissed her.

CHAPTER TEN

For the second time that evening, Rosie felt as though she were in a dream. The kind of dream where you finally get to kiss the object of your desire and he doesn't run away screaming or stare at you like you're mad. She clung to his broad shoulders, all objections forgotten, as his lips and his hard, lean body both pressed against her.

Oh. My. God.

Nothing could ever be better than this moment, she kept thinking, her eyes shut tight. Her date was in a figure-hugging tuxedo and she was in a gorgeous, skimpy party frock, and it was snowing, nearly Christmas, and she had just been eating canapés and drinking champagne at the most glamorous party she had ever gatecrashed. And now she was being kissed by this handsome part-Russian, part-assassin baker.

Then Pyotr drew her closer, and she thought, actually, maybe it *could* get better.

'Can I take you home?' he whispered against her ear, and she understood at once what he meant by that question. Not home to her nan. Home to *his bed*. Home to some wickedly pleasurable sex. His hand stroked languorously down her spine. 'Or are you planning to slap my face the instant I let you go?'

'Slap … ? No, no,' she whispered back, her cheeks flushed, her head dizzy with desire, then bit her lip. He had her confused, and all the champagne whizzing about her over-heated system was not helping. 'Erm … wait a minute. Let me think.'

Was 'no' the wrong answer? How well did she know this man, after all? Perhaps she ought to be slapping his face and screaming for help, not agreeing to everything he suggested.

Following the revelations of tonight's party in Mayfair, his contacts among important and influential Russians, his sudden and aggressive behaviour with Grigori, she ought to be wary. It was clear this man was not simply a baker, as she had innocently assumed. What else was he concealing from her? It might be risky to go to bed with him …

'Yes,' she decided firmly.

His brow creased. 'Yes … to what? The slap or the other thing?'

'The other thing.'

His brow straightened out and he smiled. 'Decided to live dangerously, have you?'

'Yes.'

He made a little noise under his breath. Then he kissed her again, and this time his tongue pressed between her lips, tasting her, probing inside. His hands roamed over her body, moulding her against him in the silky sheath dress, making his own arousal more than obvious. It was the most wildly sexy kiss she had ever experienced.

She clung to him more tightly as he lowered his head, kissing her exposed throat. 'Pyotr.'

A few moments later, when she was on the verge of collapse, her body hot and tingling with unaccustomed excitement, he finally drew back. There was a hard tinge of colour along his cheekbones and his eyes were bright. He looked as feverish and on the edge of his self-control as she felt.

'Let's grab a taxi to the train station,' he said thickly.

Rosie nodded and reluctantly released his shoulders. 'Oops,' she said, then bit her lip again, her eyes widening. 'Oh my God, I'm so sorry.'

He frowned. 'Sorry about what?'

'I completely f … forgot … ' She pointed to his right shoulder, stammering in embarrassment. His beautiful black tuxedo jacket was sticky with mincemeat and covered in flaky dots of pastry. 'When you started to kiss me, I was still holding … the m … mince pie.'

Pyotr turned his head slowly, and stared down at his own shoulder.

'Sorry,' she said again, in a small voice.

She half-expected him to say he would take her back to Nan's flat, that it was over between them, that he could not imagine himself in bed with such a klutz. But to her amazement he did none of those things.

Instead he threw back his head and gave a short, hard bark of laughter. 'My God, you're incorrigible. Do you ruin everything you touch, Rosie Redpath? No, don't answer that. I know you don't. Because there's one thing you haven't ruined tonight. That you could never ruin.'

'There is?'

Pyotr nodded, meeting her eyes. 'This,' he said softly, and kissed her again. 'Now come on, let's get back to my place. I hope you don't mind, but there are some things I need to say to you that I don't think your nan should hear.'

She stared, a little confused, then nodded. 'That's fine. I'd love to see where you live. But we won't *only* be talking, will we?'

'If you mean am I going to make love to you,' he said, holding her gaze, 'then yes. Assuming that's what you want too, of course.'

Rosie smiled, squeezing his hand and remembering too late about the remnants of mince pie on her fingers. 'Oh goodness, Pyotr. Tell me, is the Pope Catholic?'

The next morning dawned clear and cold, snow still scattered thinly across roofs and streets, gleaming in the early sunlight.

Rosie turned away from the window, wrapped in Pyotr's warm, blue dressing gown, just as the door swung open. It was the man who had spent the night with her and made love to her with such passion that he had left her confused and feeling more seduced by his charm than ever. He glanced at the empty bed, and for a moment she saw a look of panic there. Then his gaze shifted to her silent figure by the window, and that look vanished, replaced by a slow, appreciative smile.

'Your morning tea,' he murmured, and offered her a steaming mug. 'Strong, dash of milk, just as you requested.'

She came to take the mug of tea, smiling shyly at him in return. 'Thanks.'

Their eyes snagged and held a moment, then he looked her up and down. 'You look better in my dressing gown than I do,' he admitted wryly.

'You want it back?' She eyed his gorgeous bare legs, then raised her gaze past the black cotton boxers to his flat abs and muscular chest. 'Those boxer shorts are cute on you, but they don't look very practical for this kind of cold weather.'

'I'm going to grab a quick shower,' he reassured her, 'then get dressed, so don't worry about it. I have to go out again in an hour.'

'So soon?'

He had left their bed in the early hours to go to the bakery, then come back and made love to her again. Apparently he had managed to rouse Colin by phone, and asked him to come in early and get the early-baked loaves and rolls prepared for when the shop opened. It had been a lovely surprise to wake up to a large, naked man climbing over her in the semi-darkness, then kissing her sleepy body until she could not bear it any longer and begged him to make love to her.

He was certainly a stud, Rosie thought, lowering her gaze. But was he a keeper?

It was early days yet. And there was that awkward, first-morning-together feeling of intimacy and unfamiliarity between them, but behind it she could not help but remember the fierce passion of his lovemaking. He had taken them both to strange new places last night, and she could still feel the emotion trembling through her that had been the result of several cataclysmic orgasms followed by a long, soft-whispering cuddle into the early hours, both of them looking out at the stars above the dull orange glow of the cityscape.

Somewhere between bouts of lovemaking, he had told her some confused tale about his dead sister, and a long-lost niece called Anastasiya. And it was all muddled-up with the Russians she had met at the swanky party in Mayfair. But how exactly?

'Sorry.' He kissed her gently. 'Probably better if we don't go into work together anyway. Perhaps we could have lunch together, assuming I'm back in time.'

She surveyed him as he started sifting through his shirts' rack, suddenly suspicious. Was he tired of her already? She knew some men preferred one-night-stands to building a relationship. Perhaps this was his way of giving her the brush-off. If so, it would be best to know upfront. That way she could avoid making a fool of herself.

'So, are we keeping it quiet from the others?' She hesitated, seeing his frown, and tried to explain. '*This*. You and me.'

'That's up to you.'

That surprised her. 'Okay,' she agreed slowly. 'And what about the thing with your sister and ... Anastasiya?'

His back stiffened, and he turned to look at her. 'Forgive me. I shouldn't have told you about Anastasiya. It could be dangerous if you mention it to anyone else.'

'For you?'

He shook his head. 'For you, and for Anastasiya herself.'

'I won't mention it.'

'Thank you.' He threw his chosen outfit on the bed, then came across to touch her cheek. His hand was cool against her skin. Was she flushed? 'I know it's hard to take all this in, but I need you to trust me. Grigori and his family, these are not pleasant people, especially if you cross them.'

'And you think they've taken your niece?'

'Yes,' he said shortly. 'My sister made a terrible mistake when she married Nikolai. I'm sure she was in love, but he was one of them.'

'Them?'

'The Russian mafia.' He caught her arm when she began to back away. 'No, listen. It's hard to explain, but please, you must let me try.'

'Go on,' she whispered.

'When I was young, my father was a top criminal lawyer in Moscow. He was responsible for bringing many of the mafia there to justice. Then his life was threatened, and his family's too. It became too dangerous for us to remain in Russia. So he defected to America, and took us with him. It was a big step for all of us. Later we came to England when my father was defending a case here, and my sister fell in love with London ... and with Nikolai. My father tried to stop her seeing him, but she broke away from the family and married Nikolai secretly. She became pregnant with Anastasiya, and for a while, I hoped it would work out for them, that she would be happy with Nikolai.' His face was grim. 'But with his family connections, it was always going to end badly.'

'They killed her.'

Pyotr nodded. 'Yes, they killed her over some petty disagreement. They could not bear for someone with her family history to be related to them, to be part of their inner circle. In the end, I think Nikolai did try to protect her. But they killed him too. And took Anastasiya.' He shrugged. 'Perhaps as a hostage, or a bargaining chip. But whatever the reason, they never contacted my father with a ransom. Instead, the police told us she had not even been there at the time of her parents' murders. But we knew better.'

'So they kept her like, what, a *souvenir*?'

'Perhaps.' He ran a hand through his hair, looking distracted. 'Or a servant.'

Rosie was outraged. 'A servant? But she must have been so young when they killed her parents. You said … only four years old.'

'It is not uncommon for that family to groom young people for such a position. They like servants who can be trained from an early age to run errands for them. Errands they do not dare entrust to anyone outside the inner circle, but are too risky for family members.'

'That's appalling.'

He nodded. 'But it was impossible to be sure if they even had her at first. The British government refused to acknowledge that my sister might have had a young child with her at the time of her murder, so I was left to investigate on my own.'

She shook her head, speechless.

'I hired a firm of private British investigators, but with no success. Then about a year ago, when I had almost given up hope, they contacted me to say a girl matching her description and calling herself Stacey had been picked up off the streets near here. A runaway, the authorities thought. The girl was questioned but refused to give any details of her background. She was taken to the children's home across from the bakery, but disappeared after only a few weeks and was never seen again. The private investigators thought it likely the girl had been recaptured by whoever she had run away from in the first place.' He grimaced. 'By the time I got here, she had already vanished.'

Rosie's eyes widened. At last she was beginning to understand. 'That's why you started work at the bakery. Because you hoped to see her in the area again?'

'That's exactly it. At the very least I was hopeful that she might escape her captors again, and be brought back to the same place by social services, and it seemed to me that by investing in the shop I would have a legitimate reason to keep an eye on the place,' he agreed. 'But a whole year passed without another sign of her. I was beginning to despair that she was even still alive when I finally received news that she had been sighted again, this time in the company of Grigori's uncle, one of the mafia bosses. I knew then that my chance had come to get her back. I made some urgent calls, and discovered that my old friend Natalya was throwing a party.'

'And by old friend, you mean lover?'

Pyotr grimaced, his expression a little embarrassed. 'A very long time ago, yes. My student days in Moscow. But it's all water under the bridge now.'

'Looked like pretty murky water to me,' she remarked. 'Teeming with nasty bacteria, I shouldn't wonder.'

His mouth twitched. 'Jealous?'

'Not even remotely.'

'Of course not,' he agreed smoothly. 'That must be why you were so sharp with Natalya when I introduced the two of you last night.'

'I was supposed to be there as your date. I was just acting the part.'

'Yes, that was a mistake.' His jaw clenched. 'I should never have dragged you into this mess. It could become dangerous for you. But I thought we would be in and out of the party very quickly. I did not consider that, while I was trying to wring information about Anastasiya's whereabouts from Natalya, who can be a very difficult woman when she wants, you would be chatting up one of my niece's captors.'

'Sorry,' she said, without the least remorse, 'but you did

leave me alone at that party with nothing but a few mince pies for company. What was I supposed to do?'

He half-laughed, then reached for a fresh towel from his cupboard. 'Look, I need a shower. Or I'll be late.'

'You're meeting someone?'

He did not reply at first, then nodded. 'Grigori. I rang Natalya this morning, asked her to confirm our arrangement. I have certain information about their family that could see several of them arrested for fraud and murder. It's taken me many months to gather the evidence but now that I have it, I intend to use it as a bargaining tool. I'm meeting them in central London this morning. They'll hand over the girl there.'

'Let me get this straight. You get the girl back, you don't go to the police?'

'Something like that,' he agreed.

She stared. 'Are you mad? They won't hesitate, they'll kill you.'

'That's a risk I'll just have to take.'

Rosie tried to persuade Pyotr against that crazy plan for several more minutes, but he merely grew more monosyllabic, and she could tell from the stubborn tilt of his chin that she had zero chance of changing his mind.

'So where are you meeting them in central London?'

He hesitated. 'I'm going alone, Rosie. In fact, I'd rather not involve you at all in any of this. It's too dangerous. So don't bother – '

'How old is Anastasiya?' she interrupted.

'Erm … ' He blinked. 'She must be fourteen now. Why?'

'Have you any experience of teenage girls?'

'No, but – '

'Oh, I can't wait to see how you cope.' Rosie folded her arms, looking at him. 'You're planning to bring her back here?'

'I suppose so, yes.'

'Why will she sleep?'

He glanced about the bedroom, then light seemed to dawn in his face. 'Well, okay, I see your point there. This place will be a little on the small side for two people. But if I get Anastasiya back, I won't be staying here for long anyway. It wouldn't be safe.'

'And how do you think she will take to being whisked away from the only family she has ever known by a strange man?'

Pyotr stared at her. 'I am her uncle.'

'She may not know that. She may not believe you even if you can prove it. If she's like most young teenage girls, she'll try to make a break for it as soon as you take your eye off her.'

'Then I won't take my eye off her,' he stated firmly.

'You got a car?'

He shook his head, frowning. 'I don't need one in London.'

'You're bringing her home by taxi then?'

'Good luck flagging one down while holding onto a reluctant teenager.'

'I thought … ' He hesitated. 'The tube, then.'

'Oh, that will be beautiful. How many stops is it? And how many changes? No chance she'll give you the slip in one of those crowded underground stations, of course.'

He swore softly in Russian, then shook his head. 'You devil. All right, you win. I'll take you with me so you can help to look after the girl. You had better ring the cake shop and tell them … tell them you are too sick to work today.' His eyes narrowed on her face. 'But you are not to interfere. Understand? Even if things go wrong at the meeting?'

Rosie smiled, satisfied. 'Of course.'

'I'm serious. You'll head in the opposite direction and not look back if Grigori tries to double cross me?' He waited, his tone urgent. 'Promise me, Rosie. I'm not kidding about this.'

'Cross my heart and hope to die,' she swore calmly, but

with one hand behind her back, her fingers crossed. 'Oh, I'll be no trouble at all.'

CHAPTER ELEVEN

Covent Garden was cold but very Christmassy, Rosie thought, turning slowly on her heel as she checked north and south of her position. Freshly-fallen snow lay everywhere in London today, brightening the dreary city pavements, and coloured lights and stars hung across the streets, unlit for now. The day was edging towards mid-afternoon, and the sky was growing gloomier. Soon dusk would fall and the lights would come on across London, illuminating the shop windows and busy streets of the capital.

Chilly, she rubbed her arms in the over-large coat she had borrowed from Pyotr, and glanced down at her high heels. There had not been time for her to go home and change, so she was still wearing last night's sheath dress – and was bloody freezing her arse off in it! But at least the coat she had borrowed was fleece-lined, even if the arms were far too long for her.

She missed snuggling up to Pyotr in his cosy flat, remembering how had spent the night in each other's arms. She was not so naïve though as to think what they had was the start of a beautiful relationship. That is, it could be. With some spectacular luck and a sprinkle of fairy dust. But one night together was not true love, and she knew his difficult situation with Anastasiya was all either of them could think about right now.

Still, he was a fantastic lover. Not that she had much experience in the bedroom. But he had left her more than satisfied last night, and eager for more if she could get it. Which had to be a large tick on the pro side.

From her hiding place in the doorway of a shop she could see Pyotr clear across the square, waiting in the cold for the Russians to arrive. He looked lean and grim-faced and ready for action, poised on the balls of his feet, hands hanging loose by his side, constantly glancing from side to side in the crowds as though suspicious of everyone who walked past him.

Hard to believe it was the same man who had made love to her most of the night and kissed her so tenderly in the early hours of the morning.

Rosie wondered, not for the first time, if Pyotr was wise to be chasing his dead sister's child like this. What if the girl did not want to leave her new family? She was only fourteen, and for all he knew, they might have told her lies about how her parents died. Maybe even blamed it on him. Even if these people agreed to release the child in exchange for Pyotr handing over certain evidence he had complied against them, there was nothing to say she would go home with him willingly. Besides which, she must have been going to school somewhere, and have friends her own age, and possessions she did not want to leave behind. Wouldn't she be missed?

Pyotr seemed to think it would be a simple thing to take Anastasiya home – wherever 'home' was for him; she was not quite clear about that – and start a brand-new life with his niece. But she suspected he had not thought it through very carefully.

Suddenly Pyotr's face hardened.

She turned, staring in the same direction as he was. A car had pulled up at the far edge of the busy, tourist and shopper-filled square and was sitting there, engine idling. A long black limousine with blacked-out windows. The doors opened and four men climbed out, all in expensive-looking dark suits and thick overcoats, followed by a girl in jeans, scruffy trainers and a red hooded coat.

The girl's head was bent, her face drawn far back in her hood. Was she reluctant to be handed over? Rosie looked hard but could not make out the girl's expression. But she was not under restraint of any kind.

Pyotr moved forward rapidly, crossing the square towards them with long, fast strides.

Suddenly apprehensive for him and the girl, Rosie leapt out from her hiding place, meaning to follow and do what she could to ensure the hand-over went smoothly. A little warning voice in her head told her Pyotr would be cross if he knew she had come out of hiding against his explicit instructions, but she paid it no attention whatsoever. Little warning voices, she thought, needed to make more noise if they want to be taken seriously.

'Madam? Madam?' an insistent voice said at her elbow.

Her gaze fixed firmly on Pyotr's lean figure across the square, Rosie was too absorbed to listen to any of the noise and bustle around her and so did not immediately realise that the person with the high-pitched voice was speaking to her.

'Madam?'

A face popped up in front of her. A face curtained by a brightly striped cotton headscarf, and attached to a short, rotund body in an ankle-length dress.

'Please, madam?'

She dragged her gaze impatiently from Pyotr to the woman bobbing up and down in front of her. 'Yes? What do you want?'

'Mistletoe,' the woman said urgently.

'I'm sorry, I haven't got – '

'Please, please, madam,' the woman insisted, and thrust a cluster of mistletoe tied rather haphazardly with string into her face. 'Mistletoe!'

'Time,' Rosie finished, then her nose wrinkled up, her eyes closed, and she sneezed. Once. Twice, Three violent times. Afterwards she felt dazed and disorientated, and ended up staggering backwards. 'Oh my God, seriously?'

'Mistletoe, madam.'

'No thanks.'

She could not even see Pyotr through the thick green cluster of mistletoe with its little white berries that was being thrust into her face.

'Mistletoe, mistletoe,' the woman chanted, her eyes wide and appealing. 'Please buy, madam.'

Rosie sighed. It was obvious she was never going to get rid of this flower-seller without either thrusting her to the ground in an SAS-style move, which was not really something she could contemplate, or paying for the damn foliage being thrust up her nose.

'Okay, how much? How much for the mistletoe?'

'Five pounds, madam.'

Rosie stared aghast. 'Five … Are you kidding me?'

She tried to peer round the mistletoe to see what was happening with Pyotr and the girl, but the woman started waving the pale green stalks in front of her face.

'Four pounds then,' the flower-seller suggested instead in her strange, sing-song voice. 'Only four pounds for you, madam.'

'Look, I don't actually want – '

'Three pounds for you, madam. Because you nice lady.'

Rosie caught a flash of movement near where she had seen the limousine pull up, and tensed, unable to see properly. What the hell was happening over there?

She drew a sharp breath and reached into the vast pocket of Pyotr's coat for her purse. 'How much did you say? Three pounds?' She scrabbled about for the coins, then pressed them into the eager flower-seller's hands. 'There you go.'

'Thank you,' the woman said gratefully, and shoved the

mistletoe into her arms. 'Bless you, madam. Bless you.'

Rosie sneezed again, and held the mistletoe at arms' length. 'No ... problem.'

'You want plastic roses? I have plastic roses also.' The woman opened her coat wide. Inside hung several rows of thin, dusty plastic roses clipped to the material. 'A love gift for your husband.'

'No.'

'For your boyfriend?'

'No.'

Rosie tried to sidestep the infuriating woman, but the flower-seller followed her along the street, her coat still open, the plastic roses rubbing against each other.

'Your lover?'

'No, thanks. Really.'

'Your girlfriend, then?'

'My what?'

'A love gift for your girlfriend.'

'Why on earth would I want to buy – ' Then she realised the woman had been studying her huge, manly coat with shrewd eyes. 'I don't have a girlfriend. But you know what? If I did have a girlfriend, there's no way I would be buying her one of your skanky plastic roses. Now excuse me.'

'I have holly ...'

Rosie thrust the woman aside and ran across the square towards Pyotr, because she had just seen what she had feared all along. One of the Russians in the dark suits had grabbed hold of Pyotr and was now holding him, one arm twisted behind his back, while he argued with a smart-looking young man she recognised as Grigori from the party last night.

There was no sign of the girl.

'Hey,' she shouted, and the men turned in surprise as she ran towards them, dodging Christmas shoppers and nearly skidding on the slushy snow.

One of the men reached inside his jacket, staring at her

through slitty, dangerous eyes. For a gun?

Rosie was suddenly fearful she had made a terrible mistake by getting in the middle of this argument.

'No.' But Grigori held up his hand, and the man slowly withdrew his hand from inside his jacket, empty. 'Rosie,' he said quickly, and stepped away from the others to intercept her. He bowed his head rather formally, and she could have sworn he even clicked his heels together. But his polite greeting did not fool her at all, for it was obvious he was trying to deflect her. 'How nice to see you again. But I don't understand. What are you doing here?'

'You know what I'm doing here,' Rosie told him fiercely, though she had just been secretly asking herself the same question. 'Stopping you from hurting Pyotr.'

'Hurting Pyotr? Surely you are joking …'

Grigori smiled, shaking his head gently as though she had somehow understood his intentions, and glanced across at the man holding Pyotr. He must have made some kind of discreet gesture though, because the man released Pyotr's arm.

Pyotr took a quick step away from them, looking at her impatiently. His face was set and tense. 'I thought that I told you to stay out of this, Rosie.'

'Well, I didn't listen.'

'Clearly.'

'I often don't listen. It's part of my charm.'

She turned back to Grigori, her chin held high, and wondered how she had ever thought this smarmy young man attractive. Now that she knew the truth about him, she could suddenly see what had been hidden before, the sneer behind the flickering smile, the cruel eyes, the cold calculation in his face as he glanced from her to Pyotr and back again. He had a handsome face, but it was marred by a lack of genuine warmth and honesty. Grigori looked nice, he seemed nice, but underneath that carefully constructed surface he lacked the fire and raw human power Pyotr exuded with the simplest turn of his head and flash of his smile.

'Where's the girl, Grigori?' she demanded, not bothering to strive for a polite tone. 'Where's Anastasiya?'

Grigori smiled again, then shrugged delicately. 'I do not understand what you are talking about.'

'Oh, I'm sorry. Am I not making myself clear?' She hit him in the face with her clutched handful of mistletoe. 'WHERE IS ANASTASIYA?'

He staggered back, his expression one of astonishment as he shoved the bushy, green foliage away, and swore in some guttural language, presumably Russian. When she looked on, unmoved because she did not have the foggiest idea what he had said, he added for her benefit, 'What the hell was that for, you crazy bitch? First your boyfriend wants to hit me, then you try. Are you both mad?'

Boyfriend.

That sounded rather nice. She thought of the woman with the plastic roses and wondered fleetingly if she should have bought one after all.

Then the rest of what Grigori had said sank in.

'Probably.' She hit him again with the mistletoe, which was now looking a bit sorry for itself. A white berry had got mashed against his cheek, and it now dropped to the collar of his expensive dark wool overcoat. 'But I am not going to stop hitting you with this mistletoe until I see that girl again. The one who got out of the car. Where have you hidden her?'

She lifted the mistletoe again, poised to strike, but Grigori grabbed her wrist and twisted it hard so that she dropped the bent and bruised stalks in the snow. She yelped with pain and heard Pyotr swear behind her.

'Let Rosie go,' he warned Grigori, 'or I'll kill you.'

Grigori did not seem worried by that threat – not surprisingly perhaps, given that we were being constantly passed by a stream of curious shoppers, staring first at the oddly parked car, then the group of grim-looking men and the flushed woman with her teeth bared. But he let go of her wrist.

She backed away, rubbing her wrist. 'Ow. That hurt, you nasty ... prat.'

'Prat? *Prat?*'

She shrugged. 'If the cap fits.'

Rosie got the impression that Grigori, with his handmade suits and Russian mafia contacts, was not used to being referred to as a prat. *Bastard* would probably have better suited his sense of self, she considered. But she had no intention of flattering an already inflated ego by making him feel dangerous.

His previously urbane, smiling face had contorted into a snarl. 'You are meddling with things you do not understand. Because if you did, you would not be here, interfering with people who can hurt you. Badly.'

'Whoopydoo. I'm not scared of you,' she hissed.

'Then you should be.'

'Stick it up your jacksie,' she said very deliberately, then stuck out her tongue and waggled it about in his face. 'And swivel.'

His eyes bulged with disbelief. 'You ... dirty ... little ... '

'Oh, poo to you.' She kicked him in the shin. Then blew a raspberry at him. 'I'm only sorry I didn't slip a laxative into your champagne last night. And you may just have to kill me, I'm afraid, if you want to get rid of me. Because you're the one who's mad if you think we're going to walk away without what we came for.'

He hopped backwards, staring at her. 'What on earth is wrong with you?'

'I'm not sure.' She rolled her eyes together, then apart, then together again, and then made her tongue loll. 'But it might be fun to find out. If I were to start screaming and shouting like a proper crazy person, right here in Covent Garden, with all the Christmas shoppers everywhere, how long would it take before someone calls the police, do you reckon?'

His face twitched at the unpleasant mention of police, no doubt realising in the same moment that she was not bluffing.

'Very well,' Grigori growled, then pushed her aside. She nearly fell and only righted herself with difficulty. He snapped his fingers at one of the men. 'Fetch the girl.'

She looked round at Pyotr in triumphant, but he was looking away from her. His gaze was fixed on the limousine with its blacked-out windows. One of the men was bending to open the back door, speaking to someone inside, and then suddenly the girl was there again, being guided towards them by a man in a dark suit.

Under the shadowy hood of her jacket, Anastasiya looked like any normal teenage, though she was quite tall and slender for her age, almost willowy. She looked scared, sulky and withdrawn in equal measure; perhaps her teenage tendency towards gloomy introspection had been severely challenged by today's events. Her lower lip trembled as Grigori took her aside, whispered in her ear for a few minutes while she stood unmoving, her face very pale, then she was shoved towards not Pyotr but Rosie, which was a shock.

'Wait,' Grigori said sharply. He looked at Pyotr. 'I want the evidence first. As we agreed.'

Pyotr hesitated, then reached under his coat and produced a large envelope. He nodded to Rosie. 'Take her.'

Rosie took the teenage girl by the arm. 'Come on,' she whispered, and started to walk her hurriedly away across the square, which was precisely what she had arranged with Pyotr that she would do, in the eventuality that Grigori handed her over to Rosie first.

Anastasiya, who had a bulging rucksack on her back, went with her willingly enough at first. Halfway across the square though her steps began to slow, and she began throwing anxious glances back over her shoulder. 'Who ... is that man?' she asked falteringly. She sounded like a

Londoner, no trace of a Russian accent in her voice, though Rosie could see her relationship to Pyotr in the shape of her mouth and jutting chin, and in the dark luminosity of her eyes. 'And what's going to happen to him?'

'Please, just keep walking,' Rosie insisted, trying to sound calm.

But she too risked a quick glance over her shoulder, horribly concerned for the man she had begun to like rather too much.

Pyotr was surrounded by the men in suits now, his lean, dark figure almost lost in their midst.

She felt sick with apprehension. Only the memory of his instructions kept her from turning around and running back to help him, if she could. But surely the Russians would not dare to harm him in public?

It could not have been more than three o'clock, yet there were clouds darkening overhead and the chill afternoon felt like it wanted to shift into early evening. A wintry dusk was approaching, which could only be a good thing; the failing light should help to hide them from any pursuers.

Walking swiftly, they reached the brightly-lit heart of the Covent Garden shopping arcade, and there at last she felt a little safer.

Rosie's grasp of history was tenuous, at best, but she seemed to recall that there had been an old convent here, once upon a time, with extensive and well-known gardens, and the modern place name had sprung from that. She doubted there were any nuns there that afternoon, though people were milling about thickly, the small shops and exclusive boutiques thronging with shoppers while a waistcoated violinist and singer entertained people in the café area below. It sounded like the duo were performing Led Zeppelin's *Stairway to Heaven*, and clearly doing a good job; as the song finished, the crowd burst into appreciative applause, with stamps and whistles that echoed about the famous old walls of Covent Garden. The sound, bouncing off the stone ceiling, was temporarily deafening.

Rosie led the girl behind a Christmas tree hung with lights and bright baubles, fake parcels arranged about its base, and only then dared to look back properly. But in the busy crowd of shoppers, with the air thickening into dusk, she could no longer pick out the men in suits nor even see the black limousine that she knew should be parked across the square.

And there was no sign of Pyotr anywhere.

The girl turned to look at her directly, her eyes full of fear. 'Who are you? Are you here to kill me?'

CHAPTER TWELVE

'Good God, of course not,' Rosie assured her at once. 'I'm so sorry, Anastasiya. This must be very confusing and upsetting for you.' She tried to smile, though her heart was beating very hard with an unsettling mixture of panic and adrenalin. 'My name is Rosie, and I'm here to help you.'

'That man back there … '

'He's your uncle. His name is Pyotr.' She peered into the girl's confused face. 'Have you ever heard of him?'

The girl shook her head, not replying.

'His sister was your mother. Do you know … ' She hesitated, lowering her voice out of caution, even though the crowds around them were so noisy. 'Anastasiya, were you ever told what happened to your parents?'

A shuttered look came over the girl's face, and again she said nothing.

'But you know those people are not your family?'

This time the girl nodded.

'Well,' Rosie continued awkwardly, 'it's not my story to tell. Your uncle will explain the whole thing, I'm sure, if he … *when* he catches up with us. But in a nutshell, that family stole you from your true relatives when you were still very young, and your uncle has been searching for you ever since.'

'I think I guessed some of that this morning,' the girl whispered, her eyes very wide and brimming with tears, 'when Grigori told me to pack my things, that someone was coming to take me away. Someone from my *real family*.'

'You tried to run away from them once, is that right?'

She nodded. 'They found me again. Made me go back with them. After that, I was never allowed out of the house. Even when I went for a walk in the garden, I had to be accompanied.'

Rosie shook her head in horror. 'What about ... school? Did you never go?'

'Never.'

'Can you read and write?'

'Oh yes.' The girl smiled for the first time, a sad, tremulous smile. 'The old lady taught me my lessons. I can read and write in English and Russian, and I know a little history. Sometimes she brought books home from the library, and I was allowed to read them too, if they were suitable.'

'I'm glad you had one friend in that house, at least. I am sorry if you will miss her.'

The girl shrugged, her face closing up again. 'The old lady died last Christmas. I have not been allowed any books or had any more lessons since then.'

Suddenly there was a hand on Rosie's shoulder. She whirled in alarm, throwing out one arm to protect the child, ready to do battle against every single one of the Russians if necessary.

But it was not the Russians. Or rather, it was the only Russian she wanted to see at that moment.

'Pyotr!' She threw her arms about him and squeezed him hard. He smelt so damn good, she thought hungrily. So good and blessedly alive. She stopped short of licking his cheek, as that would have looked weird. 'You got away from them. I didn't think I'd ever see you again.'

'Thanks for the vote of confidence,' he said drily. 'Though if I'm honest, it was not as easy an exchange as I'd hoped. Once he had the envelope in his hand, and had checked the photographs and documents I've been collecting against this possibility, Grigori's manner changed completely. He went white with fury when he saw the photographs. He must have realised how closely my investigators have been tailing him and his people, and the kind of criminal activities they had documented on my behalf. For a moment there, I thought Grigori was planning to bundle me into his limousine and take me somewhere more private where he could … '

He stopped short, suddenly looking past her to where his niece stood, shyly waiting. 'But none of that matters now I have you back, my dear Anastasiya,' he murmured. 'At long last.'

The girl lifted her gaze to his face. 'Thank you for getting me away from them.'

'You're welcome.' He hesitated. 'I am your uncle Pyotr.'

'Pleased to meet you, Pyotr' the girl said politely, then tilted her head to one side to look enquiringly from his face to Rosie's. 'But why do you both keep calling me Anastasiya? My name is Stacey.'

He smiled. 'Anastasiya is what your mother called you. My sister. If you prefer Stacey though, that's fine. But look, we'll have time to tell you all about yourself and go through the whole family history once we've got you somewhere safe.' He glanced over his shoulder, suddenly grim-faced again. 'Grigori agreed to the exchange, to hand you over for the information I had compiled against him, but he's a dangerous man. At any minute he could change his mind and come looking for us. So we have to get out of here, and quickly.'

'To your place?'

He looked at her with dark, intense eyes. 'That could be

unwise. They may look for us there.'

She came to a decision at once. 'My place, then. No, I insist.'

'Grigori knows you. It would only be a short leap from that to finding your flat. It's too dangerous. I can't allow it.'

'Then I'm definitely going there,' she said, eyes widening, 'because my nan needs to be warned.'

He hesitated. 'Good point.'

Rosie nodded. 'All right, my place first. Then we can decide where to go afterwards. But should we take the tube or a taxi to the railway station?'

'Tube is best. I know the underground seems more exposed than grabbing a taxi. But it should keep us safer to have thousands of people around us, plus underground cameras constantly watching everything. One of Grigori's men may be watching, and it's too easy to ambush a taxi down one of these narrow side streets in central London.'

'Covent Garden tube station is probably the closest.' She looked round at their new companion with an encouraging smile, trying to make up her mind which name suited her best, Anastasiya or Stacey, and then held out her hand. 'Listen, we're going to have to run a few blocks to the tube station, which may be tricky in these heels. So I'll need your help. It's not far but we will need to move quickly.'

The girl, who was wearing trainers, looked down dubiously at Rosie's high heels and glimmering hint of a party frock, both of which must have seemed incongruous when coupled with the large, bulky coat Pyotr had lent her.

'I don't mind running.'

'I suppose you haven't had much chance for exercise though,' Rosie commented, and was pleased when the girl took her hand, 'locked up in that house for years.'

'Not at all,' Stacey said, and grinned self-consciously. 'They have a gym in the basement. I always lift a few weights and go on the treadmill or rower when I'm supposed to be cleaning the equipment. It's the only way I can keep fit.'

'Well, now's your chance to run in the open air,' Rosie told her with a smile. 'Are you ready?'

'I think so.'

Pyotr reached out and took the girl's other hand, so she would be sandwiched safely between them while they made their way to the nearby Covent Garden tube station.

'Then let's run,' he said.

It was fully dark by the time they got back to the small, modestly decorated flat Rosie Redpath shared with her grandmother, and Pyotr was glad to have his niece safely off the streets and in his care at last.

The old lady looked surprised to see them with a pale, undernourished teenage girl trailing over the threshold behind Rosie. But she had had no unexpected visitors, Nora told them, which relieved his mind.

Rosie settled the girl on the couch, then knelt to switch on the electric heater, as the living room was chilly.

Pyotr made straight for the window and twitched the closed curtains back a crack, peering down through the gap into the car park below. There was no sign of any unusual activity, no lights turning down from the nearby main road, and the thin layer of snow nearest the entrance showed only their own footprints. It would appear as though most people in the block were staying in on this dark December evening, or perhaps staying out until later.

He felt a sense of relief that they did not seem to have been followed, and allowed himself a brief flicker of triumph too. He had not been afraid when Grigori threatened to execute him, but it had occurred to him that Rosie would be ill-equipped to protect his niece from the Russians if he were to die.

That had made him angry. And anger had saved him. 'I left details of this meeting with my father,' he had lied, looking Grigori straight in the eye. 'and he will know how to act if I am never seen alive again.'

Grigori had not liked that. His jaw had clenched, then he had motioned his heavies to step aside and let him go free. 'I won't forget about this,' he had said softly, and come closer to Pyotr, saying for his ears only, 'so if I were you, I would leave London. Leave England, in fact. And take your sister's brat with you. Because if I find either of you on our patch again … ' He had made an abrupt gesture with his gloved hands, like snapping the neck of a turkey, then sneered as he walked away to his car. 'Merry Christmas to you and yours, Pyotr.'

Nora was a little flustered, he could see that. Arms folded in an obvious sign of disapproval, she was talking quietly to her granddaughter. 'But you were out all night,' she was saying. 'I was worried sick.'

'Sorry, Nana.'

'It's not like you to do that to me. I mean, I know you're a grown woman now, and you must do as you please. I'm not cross. But next time, do give me a quick call before you disappear without warning.'

'There won't be a next time,' Rosie said stoutly, then glanced across at him.

Pyotr frowned and let the curtain drop. *There won't be a next time.*

He wondered what she meant by that. Their night together had been the most sensuous, satisfying experience he had enjoyed for many years; it had shaken him to wake up beside her and remember their passionate lovemaking with an ache in his heart, he could not deny it.

He had not wanted last night to end. But of course he had know the end was surely inevitable. He had succeeded in getting his sister's long-lost daughter back; now it must be his life's task to protect her, and to raise her as he felt his sister would have done, in loving safety.

Which meant taking the girl far away from here. Until he had Anastasiya's official papers sorted out, they would be unable to leave the United Kingdom and join his parents in America. He had hopes of finding them a place to live in the depths of the countryside. Somewhere quiet where they could start again without constantly looking over their shoulders for Grigori to find them.

But Rosie would not want to leave London. She had dreams and ambitions, she had admitted as much to him. She was still young, he must remind himself of that whenever he looked at her with longing in his soul. She was so full of life and energy, ready for an exciting career out there in the world, and she deserved to put her skills to better use than was possible in the cake shop.

He could not take her away from the city with him and Anastasiya. It would be unfair on a young woman whose life was just starting.

So what had been so pleasurable and startlingly intimate last night was doomed to end in only a few hours, and in a farewell he had frankly not expected to make. It had always been a strong possibility that the exchange would fail, and he would be killed by Grigori. The risk had seemed worth the reward at the planning stage. Now though, the reality of his sacrifice was clear. The relationship that had been slowly growing between him and Rosie had blossomed into sudden fire last night, but now must end just as abruptly.

Perhaps she had not enjoyed last night as much as he had though. *There won't be a next time.* That hurt him, the unexpected pain catching him off guard, and he cleared his throat before speaking, surprised by the impact of her words.

'I'm sorry to say we won't be able to stay here longer than one night,' he told his niece, somehow managing a smile as he approached her. The poor child must have been terrified by today's events; she would hardly be thrilled to hear this grim, unfamiliar uncle would be whisking her away so soon.

Rosie looked at him, startled. 'You're leaving so soon?'

'I want to put as much distance between my niece and

Grigori as possible. It's likely he won't bother pursuing us. But I'm not going to gamble on that.' He shook his head. 'No, it's best if we leave London tomorrow morning. Head far north. In fact, I've been looking into getting a place up in Scotland, and I have some contacts up there. That should be far away enough to keep us off Grigori's radar.'

Nora pursed her lips. 'Running away? That doesn't sound like a good idea.'

'Sometimes running away is the best option,' he said drily. 'These are dangerous people and they dislike being crossed. You can't reason with them. And I've no desire to spend the next ten years looking over my shoulder.'

Anastasiya nodded, looking relieved. 'I agree with my uncle,' she said simply. 'Let's get out of London. He's right, it's not safe for us here.'

Nora's eyes widened. 'Well, I like my flat and – '

'I only meant me and Anastasiya,' he said flatly, and drew in a slow breath when a sudden silence fell in the room. He did not look at Rosie, though he could sense her gaze on his face. 'Sorry, my mind's made up.'

'So that's it?' Rosie asked, her voice unrevealing.

He forced himself to nod. It hurt to break it off, more deeply than he had expected it would, but it was important to do this cleanly. Not to build up any hopes that their newfound relationship could survive this break.

'Yes, that's it.'

Rosie said nothing for a moment, then muttered, 'Fine, whatever,' and left the room, slamming the door behind her.

No one said anything.

The door opened again and Rosie looked in at them all, her face flushed, then she went back out, slamming the door a second time.

'That's me being cross,' she announced loudly through the closed door.

'We got the point first time, love,' her grandmother agreed, arms still folded.

The other two turned to look at him.

'What?' Pyotr asked them, a little bewildered by the accusation in both their gazes. He frowned, not sure what had just happened. 'I thought it best to be honest.'

'Oh yes, that was a very good idea,' Nora said drily.

The girl shook her head. 'You need to go after her. Right now. And say sorry. And tell her she can come too.'

'But – '

Anastasiya had folded her arms too, and now sat back on the sofa, crossing her legs. She raised her eyebrows, staring back at him in a way that reminded him eerily of his sister at the same age. 'Better hurry up, Uncle Pyotr,' she told him. 'Or she may never forgive you.'

'You want her to come with us?'

She nodded simply. 'I don't think I could live with you on my own. Can you cook?'

He stared. 'Of course I can cook. I'm a professional baker.'

'Yes, you told me that on the train. But can you cook *dinner*?' She made a face when Pyotr said nothing, scratching his head and mentally running through a list of items he could cook only to realise that, actually, his range in the kitchen was a little limited. 'Uhuh. I thought so. Which means I'll be doing all the cooking and cleaning within five minutes of moving in with me, and then I might as well be back at Grigori's house, slaving every hour for him and his family.'

Nora gasped. 'Doing *what*?'

'I've been their servant ever since I was old enough to be put to work,' Anastasiya told the old lady in a trembling voice, and now he could see a single tear rolling silently down her cheek. 'I was forced to fetch and carry for them at first, and then to clean the house and do all the laundry, and even look after the younger children once they decided I could be trusted with that too. And if I ever refused to do my work, or made a mistake, I was punished.'

'They hit you?' Nora demanded, her voice quivering with outrage.

The girl shook her head reluctantly. 'No, they weren't that cruel. But they would take away my books, and sometimes lock me in my room and refuse me food.' She hesitated. 'And Grigori scared me. The way he would look at me sometimes … '

Nora sat next to her on the sofa and took the girl in her arms. 'There, there,' she said comfortably, and drew the girl against her ample breasts, 'you let it all out. You're safe now, and we're not going to let those horrible people near you again.' She looked up at Pyotr through narrowed eyes. 'Are we?'

'No,' Pyotr agreed.

He was shaken by what his niece had said, even though he had suspected that, wherever she was, she was not being well-treated. But this was beyond what he had thought possible. What kind of appalling abuse had this child faced, year after year, growing up in captivity?

No wonder she had tried to run away, perhaps more than once, and been too scared to tell anyone about what she had suffered.

He ought to involve the police and the social services. Then Grigori and his family could be made to pay for their crimes against his niece. But of course there would be an inevitable cover-up, followed by bloody reprisals, and their lives would not be worth living after it was all over, assuming they made it that far unscathed.

No, Grigori and his family had too many important people in their pockets. If they could get away with murder, which he knew they had already done more than once, they could certainly get away with the long-term enslavement of a Russian-born girl who had never officially been missing.

Nora was glaring at him over the top of the girl's head. When he met her gaze, surprised, she rolled her eyes towards the door, then back again.

He frowned. 'Are you all right?'

Again the old lady rolled her eyes to the door, then screwed up her mouth like she was kissing the air.

'I'm sorry,' he said, totally bewildered by her bizarre and contorted expressions, 'I don't quite – '

'Go after her,' she said crossly, interrupting him. 'Go after Rosie. Say you're sorry. Give the poor girl a nice kiss.' She shook her head. 'Men these days … I sometimes think you all need to be spoonfed.'

He felt a hard flush in his cheeks at this accusation, and did not immediately move. Who was she to interfere? Then he thought of Rosie's expression when she left the room, and saw the concern in her grandmother's face, and felt something inside him shift painfully. Yes, Rosie was angry with him, and that rankled, he could not deny it. But she was angry for a good reason. He had slept with her last night, and now it must look like he was trying to throw her aside without any proper explanation.

'Would you like a nice slice of Christmas cake?' Nora asked his niece, glancing down into her tear-stained face.

The girl muttered something indistinct.

'Now, that's not very nice. You must have had some pretty rubbish Christmas cake in the past if you think it tastes like shoe leather dipped in rum' the old lady said stiffly, but then smiled. 'I know. How about some chocolate Yule log?'

Anastasiya hiccupped, then nodded jerkily.

'There,' Nora said with obvious satisfaction, nodding, and gave Pyotr a significant sideways look. 'I've found there are few disasters in life that can't be made better with a large slice of cake.'

A touch chagrined, Pyotr smiled his gratitude at Nora, then left his niece in the older woman's experienced hands, closing the door behind him quietly. Anastasiya was still shaken and upset by what had happened today and in her past, that was obvious. But she would be fine for a while with Rosie's grandmother, he felt sure of it. Perhaps Nora reminded her of the old lady who had died, the one who taught her to read and write, and brought her books from the library.

If only he could make the girl feel that comfortable with him too.

Rosie was in her cluttered bedroom, lying on her back on the bed and staring up at the ceiling. She had changed out of the shimmering dress he had bought her – it was dangling from a pink lampshade as though she had tossed it aside in a temper – and was in a pair of blue-and-white striped pyjamas. It looked as though she had been crying.

She did not sit up or look at him when he came in, though it was clear from her sudden stiffness that she knew he was there.

'Rosie,' he said softly.

She ignored him.

He stood beside the bed, looking down at her gorgeous, lithe body and trying not to remember her naked. But it was hard. Or more correctly, he was. Without meaning to be. He closed his eyes briefly, willing himself to think of her future, to imagine how depressed she would become if he persuaded her to leave London and abandon her dreams of becoming a big shot caterer, maybe owning her own firm one day. He had not forgotten what she had told him that first day. And he wanted those things for her too. Unfortunately he also wanted her in his bed, and the two were simply not compatible. Not anymore, not now that he was responsible for Anastasiya's welfare.

Down, boy! he thought crossly.

'When will you leave?' she asked in a thin, brittle voice, still staring at the ceiling.

'First light.'

She nodded, then turned away, hugging her pillow.

'Rosie, you know this can't work,' he told her bluntly. 'You need to be here in London for your career. I have to take that girl somewhere Grigori will never think to look. Somewhere remote and unpopulated. There wouldn't be any opportunities there for you to shine, and I think you deserve a chance to show the world what you can do. Which means staying here and not coming with us.'

'Idiot,' she said thickly.

'I'm sorry?'

'Plonker.'

He felt his jaw clench. 'Now listen – '

'No, you listen.' She sat up and glared at him, her face still flushed, her eyes red from where she had been crying. 'You think I care a stuff about any of that crap? I like Anastasiya. I want to help her.'

'This would mean changing your whole life.'

'No, just where I live.' She shook her head, holding his gaze. 'I can't believe how casual you're being about this. I thought we connected. More than that, I thought we were like mates. That what we experienced last night was worth risking my life for. That's why I went with you today. And that's why I'm willing to come with you now.'

'I thank you for what you did today. You were right, I could never have got Anastasiya back with your help. That doesn't mean it's right for you to go any further down this road with me.'

'What we did last night was fantastic,' she continued blithely, ignoring what he had said, 'it was the best sex I've ever had. But I'm not sailing away on a cloud of bliss, thinking you must want to marry me now or anything – '

'I do, actually,' he said sharply, interrupting her in his turn.

'Well, of course, you would say that,' she exclaimed, and shook her head dismissively. Her look was withering, her tone acidic. 'Now that you know I'm not bothered.'

'If you're not bothered, as you claim, why have you been sulking in here for the past fifteen minutes?'

'I have not been sulking.'

He gestured to her reddened eyes. 'Crying, then. Or

have you been chopping onions?' He glanced about the bedroom before adding sarcastically, 'Because I don't see any.'

Again Rosie ignored him, angrily flicking her hair out of her eyes. He thought she looked more beautiful than ever, all fired-up with energy and determined to put him in his place. 'I know that just because we scorched the sheets last night, it doesn't mean we're destined to be together forever.'

'True enough. But I suppose we could do worse than give it a go.'

'All the same, I thought we might ... ' She stopped in the middle of her rant, staring up at him. 'Wh .. what did you say?' Her voice became a squeak. 'And ... you want to m ... marry me?'

Pyotr sat beside her on the bed, unable to resist giving in to the dangerous temptation he had been fighting ever since he walked into her homely little bedroom with its clutter and teddy bears and quirky, blue, tie-dye bedspread. He slipped an arm about her waist and drew her close, breathing in her scent.

'I said, I love you,' he whispered, then bent his head to kiss her lips.

Her lips parted, and her arms rose, linking behind his neck. Then she drew him down onto the bed and they lay together for a while, touching and kissing each other in a kind of mesmeric fever. Their hands met at hip-level and held fast, fingers interlacing. He thought he had never before experienced such intimacy with another human being, nor known such a powerful sense of love and trust.

'It's too soon for all this,' she whispered, staring at him.

'You don't want it?'

'No, I want it. Oh my God, I want it. It's just ... I'm always searching for ways to be sure of what I want, while you are the opposite. How can you feel like this so soon? How can you be so *sure* of yourself?'

'As soon as I met you, Rosie Redpath, I knew things

would be different with you. You stopped me in my tracks.
You made me want you just by smiling.'

'You're sure that wasn't just indigestion? Nan says too
many cream cakes can do funny things to a person.'

'I'm in love with you,' he told her firmly, then kissed
her again, holding her close while his lips caressed hers.
There was silence between them for a few more minutes,
then he spoke quietly against her warm throat. 'And I want
to marry you. Why wait now that I've found my perfect
partner? Besides, I can't imagine spending my life with
anyone else but you.'

'Oh Pyotr,' she murmured through swollen lips.

'Darling.'

'I think I probably love you too. Is that … crazy?'

'Not even slightly.'

Pyotr stared into her heavy-lidded eyes, and suddenly
realised he had no idea how much time had passed since
they started kissing. He was shocked and could not believe
his lack of discipline. He had only come in here to check
she was okay, and to say goodbye. But then he had seen
her flushed face and tears in her eyes, and heard the
tremor of emotion in her voice, and his heart had squeezed
hard, like a fist in his chest, until he thought it would burst
with pain.

What the hell had happened to his famous self-control?
To his determination that she should not suffer because of
his need to get Anastasiya away to safety?

He made an effort to regain control.

'Still, I must not be selfish about this. If you come with
us, you might be ruining your life. I can't let you throw
your career away.'

'My career. My choice.'

He closed his eyes. 'Okay, well, perhaps we could open
a shop up there in Scotland. A cake shop. Or a catering
business. Under a false name. I'm not bad as a baker, it
turns out, even though it was only a cover while I looked
for Anastasiya. Perhaps it's time I made something real out

of those skills.'

'Yes, yes. And Nan must come too, if I can persuade her. She's a great cake maker.'

He mused. 'We could sell traditional Russian cakes to the locals.'

'And chocolate eclairs and mince pies.'

'And cream horns.'

'And apple pie,' she agreed, grinning. 'And Christmas cake.'

'And a mini-Yule log with an earring inside it.'

She stopped at that extraordinary remark, looking back at him in a stunned silence, her smile wiped away. She turned pale, then flushed again, then finally whispered, 'How did you … ?'

'Mrs Minchin sent me a text. A series of texts, actually. She says we nearly lost one of our regular customers.'

Her eyes were huge. 'Who?'

'The woman in the shop opposite,' he told her calmly. 'Diana.'

'Diana.'

'Luckily her husband knew the Heimlich Manoeuvre, and she's a good sport. An old friend of Mrs Minchin's. She nearly choked to death on your earring. However, she's decided not to sue and accepted a year's worth of free apple strudel in return.'

She covered her face in her hands. 'Oh my God. I'm so sorry.'

He laughed and kissed her fingers. 'Don't worry. You didn't kill anyone. This time. But perhaps now you understand why we don't allow staff to wear jewellery while preparing food.'

'I'm such an idiot. Is Mrs Minchin *very* angry?'

'But you're a beautiful idiot. And Mrs Minchin isn't just angry, she's livid. She says you're sacked.'

Her mouth widened, horror in her face. 'Oh no.'

'Hey, don't look like that. It doesn't matter, you don't need that job. I've told her I'm not going back either. She can run the shop on her own from now on. I don't need to be there under cover anymore, not now I've found Anastasiya.' He smiled drily. 'Coming from a wealthy family like mine has its advantages. I'll stay on as her silent partner, but she can hire a new baker instead to do the physical labour.'

She sighed. 'I've made such a mess of my first job.'

'It hasn't been pretty at times,' he agreed with a grin. 'But I still love you and I'd be happy to take you on as my partner if I ever open my own bakery. So don't go changing, okay? Even if it means you have to kill a few customers along the way. I can always get more customers. But I fear *you* would be impossible to replace, Rosie Redpath.'

She lowered her hands, staring at him, wide-eyed. Her lip trembled. 'I think that's the loveliest thing anyone has ever said to me,' she said in a hoarse voice. 'Make love to me, please.'

'Right now?"

She nodded, her face aglow with desire.

He looked back at her and remembered his teenage crush, Marina, the girl he had loved so deeply and desperately. He had wanted to die when she ran away from home with a young soldier, never to be seen again. He had remained wrapped up in his misery over Marina for years, even when dating other women, like the duplicitous Natalya. It had seemed impossible that he would ever replace her in his heart. That first day when Rosie came to the shop and he had spoken to her, something about her had reminded him of Marina. The determined way she held herself, perhaps, or a flicker of humour about her mouth and eyes, or perhaps the wilful slant of her chin. That resemblance had sparked his interest in this woman, and made him desire her more than perhaps he should have done, given that she was his employee.

Now though, he could barely remember what Marina had looked like. His love for Rosie had long since eclipsed that old nostalgic memory of his youth; now it was only her face he dreamt about in the darkest hours of the night. Her face – and her lush, delectable body, he thought hungrily.

'Your nan and my niece are in the kitchen right now, eating chocolate cake and probably listening to everything that's going on in here,' he pointed out drily. 'Much as I love you, I doubt that I could adequately … *perform* under those circumstances. But I'm willing to give it a go if you insist.'

Rosie hesitated, looking tempted, then shook her head. 'No,' she said more firmly, 'no, you're right. It would be horribly embarrassing if one of them was to walk in on us. Besides, I must find a place for poor Anastasiya to sleep – she looks just like you, did I say? – and make sure my nan trundles off to bed too, bless her. Then we'll sneak back in here together and …'

'Set off the smoke alarm?' he suggested, amused by the wicked glint in her eyes.

She kissed him lingeringly, her lips pliant and inviting, and he had to pull away in the end, suddenly breathless and intent.

'Something like that,' Rosie agreed, and ran her tongue along her lips as she eyed him speculatively. 'I do hope you're feeling energetic.'

'For you, always,' he promised her.

EPILOGUE

It was Christmas Eve and the remote, Scottish village was glittering with lights under a thick, silent blanket of snow, for all the world like one of his Christmas window displays back at the bakery. The sky above them was a stunning pitch-black, only constellations visible to the horizon, stars picked out in absolute clarity like diamonds on a black velvet display, no dull orange city glow to mask their natural beauty. Pyotr drew in a deep breath, revelling in the stillness and quiet of this rural scene. For a moment he was reminded of the snowy countryside around Moscow during those long Russian winters, and felt a stab of nostalgia. Though there was nowhere on earth he would rather be than here with this woman by his side. There was a woody smell on the air from the smoking village chimneys, and a fresh scent of pine needles on his jumper from where he had just been rearranging the angel on top of the real Christmas tree in the living room of their cottage.

'Left a bit,' Nora had said, directing him as he perched on top of a stepladder, 'no, right a bit now. To the left again. There, that's perfect.'

With the angel in perfect position, Anastasiya – or

Stacey as she preferred to be called – had switched on the Christmas lights, and they had all stood back to admire the effect. Which had been pretty impressive, he had to admit. Tinsel and baubles with tiny hand-wrapped presents and wooden stars decorated the tree's thick, green branches, while its heady scent of pine filled every room of the cottage. Now, with the festive lights switched on and winking amidst the tinsel, it was clear that Christmas really had arrived.

Standing beside him in the chilly evening air, also admiring the view across the valley and the village nestling at its base, Rosie stirred. 'I'm glad we picked this place. It may be a couple of hours' drive to civilization, but it's so beautiful here.'

'Isn't it?' He slipped an arm about her waist, which was not as easy to do as when they first made love. 'Feeling better, darling?'

'Much better, thanks. They say the nausea tails off after the first ten weeks.'

'If it's a boy.'

'That's an old wives' tale.'

'Well,' he pointed out, ' you are an old wife now.'

She shoved him crossly. 'Oh, you!'

He laughed, but did not release her. 'I love you,' he said softly.

'I love you too,' she whispered back.

'I'm sorry it took me so long to get the tree up. I'll manage things better next year, when it's not so crazy.'

'You think things will be easier next Christmas?'

He shrugged. 'Getting the new business up and running has been a real time-consumer these past few months. I'm just glad we've got a chance to stop and spend time together for a few days over Christmas.'

'And next year, we'll have Baby underfoot,' she reminded him.

He drew a breath, then said nothing, too stunned with the reality of what she was saying to respond.

'Looking forward to being a dad?' she asked, and her smile did nothing to mask her anxiety.

'Of course I am,' he reassured her, and bent to kiss her generous mouth. His eyes closed as they kissed, and he felt a wonderful, deep contentment. Not only had they left the worries of London and Grigori far behind, but Rosie and he had more than bonded over the need to resettle in Scotland, falling head-over-heels in love with each other. The kind of love, he thought, that lasts a lifetime.

Which was why he had married her that summer. And now they were expecting their first child. Life really could not be much sweeter.

Rosie drew back from her husband's kiss, admiring his handsome profile in the dark as he turned to look back up at the stars. There was such conviction in his voice, it laid the last of her fears to rest.

Life could not be much more perfect for them, she thought, and rested a hand gently on the bump under her woollen dress. She had no idea what the future would hold, but she was content to wait and see, with Pyotr by her side. And their new business was almost as exciting as the baby growing inside her, a catering business for their region devoted to cakes for special occasions. The rush for Christmas trade had swept both of them off their feet, and Nora had plunged into the fray to help them, even teaching Stacey how to ice and decorate Christmas cakes.

'Did you see Stacey earlier?' she asked, amused by a sudden memory. 'With the piping bag? Nan was showing her how to draw shapes and write letters with icing. She left it on the kitchen chair, then sat down on it by accident. The icing shot out and hit the cat in the face!'

'That girl ... ' But he was laughing. 'She reminds me so much of my sister, always getting into trouble.'

'But she's settled in well at the school.'

'Yes,' he agreed, and a note of consternation crept into his deep voice. 'Though she's forever on the phone these days.'

Rosie grinned in the darkness, but did not tell her husband what she and Nan suspected, which was that Stacey had started going out with one of the local boys, a quiet, dark-haired lad whose father was a farmer. Hence all the late night phone calls and texts. Pyotr would freak out and get all ridiculously over-protective if he knew. That might risk alienating the girl, who had only just begun to relax into her new life up here in rural Scotland.

'That's teenager girls for you,' she told him lightly.

Snow began to fall around them again, a few wayward flakes melting on the woolly sleeve of Pyotr's cheerful Christmas jumper. She had almost never seen snow at Christmas in London, and she still never tired of seeing the picture postcard-style view across the valley, of white roofs and roads and trees, and the bright sheen of Christmas lights in every window.

But the evening was growing distinctly chilly, and when Rosie shivered, her husband looked down at her with dark, gleaming eyes. 'You're cold. Time to go inside. I need to light the fire, and I have a sudden hankering for a slice of your nan's delicious Christmas cake.'

'She does has a talent for Christmas cakes.'

He agreed, then mused, 'And one you seem to have inherited. I nearly broke my molar on a five pence coin in that Christmas pudding she made for us last year.'

She looked up, blushing at his significant look, and remembered the earring she had once inadvertently dropped into a Yule log.

'It's traditional,' she said defensively. 'The Victorians used to stir a sixpence into the plum pudding mix, didn't they? Don't be so mean.'

'I'm trying not to be. But I hope she hasn't slipped any coins or surprise trinkets into this year's pudding. I value my teeth even if she doesn't.'

'Pyotr,' she said softly.

'Mmm?'

'Merry Christmas.'

He grinned then, relenting a little, and bent to kiss her lips. She clung to him, absurdly happy. 'Merry Christmas, darling,' he whispered in her ear, then held her tight.

She listened to the quickening thud of his heart and could not imagine herself being anywhere but in this house, in his arms, secure in his love.

'Come on,' he said eventually, straightening to look out across the glittering lights of the village one more time, 'let's go and rescue Stacey from your grandmother. Those two together seem to add up to trouble. Teaching her how to ice cakes is one thing ... but just before I came out to find you, I overheard Nora challenge the poor girl to a dance contest.'

'So? What's wrong with that?' Rosie demanded, instantly ready to defend her quirky nan against any further accusations. 'Nan's an excellent dancer.'

'I'm sure she is, my love.' Pyotr looked at her sardonically. 'The only thing is, at the time your grandmother issued this challenge, she was wearing a lampshade on her head and standing on the kitchen table.'

'She did say earlier that she was gearing up for the Christmas edition of *Strictly Come Dancing*,' Rosie admitted, then caught his eye and giggled.

Beth Good was born and raised in Essex, England, then whisked away to an island tax haven at the age of eleven to attend an exclusive public school and rub shoulders with the rich and famous. Sadly she never became rich or famous herself, so had to settle for infamy as a writer of dubious novels.

Starting out as an impoverished poet, Beth has been writing and publishing fiction since 1998, and no longer has to rely on a string of husbands to pay her bills. She writes both contemporary and historical fiction under various pseudonyms including Jane Holland, Victoria Lamb, Elizabeth Moss and Hannah Coates. Her work is both traditionally and independently published. Her latest publication as Jane Holland is a fast-paced psychological thriller: Girl Number One.

Beth currently lives in the West Country where she spends a great deal of time thinking romantic thoughts while staring out of her window at sheep. (These two activities are unrelated.)

Printed in Great Britain
by Amazon